113503

113503

Trail of the Long Riders

TRAIL OF THE LONG RIDERS

LEE MARTIN

AVALON BOOKS
THOMAS BOUREGY AND COMPANY, INC.
401 LAFAYETTE STREET
NEW YORK, NEW YORK 10003

PRINTED IN THE UNITED STATES OF AMERICA
BY HADDON CRAFTSMEN, SCRANTON, PENNSYLVANIA

To my brother Jack, who ropes, rides, and sings with the best, and to his lovely wife, Ruby, who keeps him smiling.

Chapter One

IT was the fall of 1877 in the new state of Colorado. This had been a shorter drive on the cattle trail from Texas, but it had been one of the toughest. In camp that night on the treeless plain, the men were exhausted and weary from the stampede and slowly taking to their blankets. But Jess Darringer sensed that more trouble was coming.

Standing near the fire where the burning chips had a pungent smell, he pushed his wide-brimmed Stetson back from his hard, clean-shaven face. His square jaw was set below his gleaming steel-gray eyes. Warm in his leather coat, he turned as the gruff foreman approached.

"Jess, there's a young feller been waitin' in camp for you. Claims he's your half brother."

Surprised, Jess turned to watch the young stranger approach from out of the night. Just twenty-seven, Jess had been on the cattle trail

1

for four years, and he had developed an instinct for trouble, like now.

The youth was a Darringer all right, a younger Jess. He was tall, with the same square jaw and slight hook of the nose, collar-length brown hair, broad shoulders, and the same easy way of moving. Wool jacket open, six-gun exposed, wearing stiff new Levi's, he was in his mid-twenties, one of their mother's second brood. His dark eyes were brown instead of gray.

When Jess and his three brothers left home, it had been because their widowed mother had married their father's cousin within a year, another Darringer but not as agreeable. The new youngsters were a real headache, and the ranch became too crowded.

"Sam Darringer," the fellow said.

They shook hands and were silent as they approached the chuck wagon. Jess remembered Sam as the most devilish of his half brothers. They filled tin cups with black coffee and walked to the edge of the firelight, away from the sleeping men. The glow cast their shadows on the cold night.

"You oughta be about twenty-five," Jess said.

"Sure am."

"Somethin' wrong in Texas?"

"Ma's fine. The family's fine."

Jess was tired, and his legs were like adobe

posts, ready to crumble. He didn't want to hear any bad news. He just wanted to lie down and go to sleep. But he was glad to see Sam. It was a touch of home.

"How's your pa?" Jess asked.

"Oh, buying up every bit of land he can get his hands on. Got my brothers and sisters workin' hard. He's bound and determined to own half of Texas."

"And you?"

"Me? I got a restless foot. I've read everything you've written to Ma. About the stampedes, the buffalo, the tall tales around the campfire."

"That why you're here?"

"No," Sam said, kicking at the dirt.

"Well, spit it out."

"You remember Sue Ellen Cambridge?"

Jess went warm all over, clear into his boots. Remember her? Four years ago he had been plenty close to popping the question, but his yearn to wander had pulled him away. He had said good-bye, never expecting to return, but even now, he could see her curly blond hair and those clear blue eyes. Still, he didn't regret his freedom. She had wanted a gentle city life while he loved to live off the land.

Sue Ellen was probably getting married. That was why Sam was here. Well, Jess was sad but also mighty happy for her. Relieved, he grinned at Sam.

"Is that why you came all this way?" he asked.

Sam shrugged. "I brung you a letter from Ma."

"Why didn't you say so?"

Jess held out his hand as Sam reluctantly surrendered the letter. Moving closer to the firelight, Jess set his cup down. The envelope was sealed. He tore it open, recognizing their mother's neat hand as he unfolded the pages and some kind of receipt. He missed her, wanted to squeeze her tiny body and plant a big kiss on her brow. As he read, he could almost hear her voice.

Dear Jess,

It is with sadness that I must write this to you, but you are the only son who doesn't lose his temper. You're the son who loves music and books.

Sue Ellen Cambridge never married. She was living alone in that cottage and teaching school. Last July, some bad men came her way, and she was murdered. They took her silver locket with her initials and a small wooden music box that played "Shenandoah."

The only thing that was found was this piece of paper, a receipt for ten dollars. It was out by the corral. It's not dated and doesn't say what it was for, but it was made out to "Colby" from a saddlery called Morley's in Buzzard's Creek, Colorado. We're told there's a large clan of these Colbys.

Jess didn't believe what he was reading. It made him sick to his stomach. His lips were drawn tight over his teeth. He read on.

That's all I can tell you, Jess. They think it was four or five men riding north in the night. No one could follow their trail. She has no kin to help.

It was hard for Jess to grasp. He kept staring at the letter and the faded, handwritten receipt. His weary body had regained energy, and he was seething. He forced himself to read further, his eyes burning.

Your brother Ben is a lawyer now and expecting his first child. Your brothers Clay and Henry are waiting for the pardons Ben has arranged. It's important they stay out of trouble.
Jess, I don't know who can help you, but I know I can trust you, of all my sons, to keep your gun in your holster. If you must, just find these men and have them arrested.

*Please send Sam home. He is too much
like your brothers.*
God bless you, Jess.

Love,
Mother

After reading the pages a second time, Jess folded them slowly with the receipt, placed them in the envelope, and shoved it inside his leather jacket. Yes, he loved music, especially his new concertina, and he read every book he could find. But he was also a Darringer, a fast gun.

"You know what's in it?" Jess asked.

"Yeah, and I understand you're delivering this herd to a buyer in Colorado. That means you can ride in a day or two."

Sam stood with his hand resting on his six-gun, holster set low on his right hip. He was the picture of a young Darringer, ready to ride and fight.

Jess thought of his own Army Colt .45 under his coat. Just this last spring, he had fought in an Arizona range war with his brothers, but he was not a fighting man by nature.

He saved most of his wages and was planning to have his own spread, but he kept putting it off because he liked the winters when he could wander alone and unhindered.

Now the long rest he had hoped to enjoy was

turning into a manhunt, a bitter and haunting one.

The cook poured them the remainder of the thick, black coffee. As the little man set about closing his shop, Jess and Sam wandered to the edge of the firelight, where they gazed into the cold, dark night. They could hear the distant singing of the night riders.

Some of the men were snoring softly. Every man was weary to the bone. Even the cattle were not bellowing as usual.

"Sorry about Sue Ellen," Sam said. When Jess didn't answer, he changed the subject. "I heard there was a stampede."

"Early this morning," Jess replied. "Lost five head and my good swimmin' horse."

Jess looked away, sipping his coffee. He didn't want Sam to see the tears in his eyes. He had loved that old black. It had bitten him often and would swell up when he'd try to tighten the cinch, but it had saved his life more than once. He swallowed and continued the story.

"We had crossed the river and were restin' the herd. About that time, three old buffalo bulls tangled with the remuda. Nothin' gets a horse to buckin' and runnin' like the smell of buffalo."

"That set off the stampede?" Sam asked.

"Cattle and all. They didn't stop till we got to Colorado. While we were tryin' to round 'em off, Rocher, one of the old-timers, plowed right into me, and my horse fell into the herd. I got clear by jumpin' up with Rocher. My horse didn't make it."

"But at least you did."

"Don't feel much like it," Jess said wearily. He didn't want to think about the stampede or about what had happened to Sue Ellen. He just wanted to sleep.

Sam rested his hand on his holstered six-gun. His dark eyes gleaming with curiosity, he glanced over at Jess's gun belt, mostly hidden by the leather coat.

"Tell me, Jess, are you fast on the draw?"

"As much as any, I reckon."

"Well, I'm fast as a whistle. You're gonna need me when you go after those men."

"Ma wants you home."

"She put that in there?" Sam asked, shuffling his weight as he downed his coffee. "Why, she won't let me cross from the house to the barn. I want to get out and breathe some life in me. I got to see some buffalo while they're still some left. I want to get up in the Shining Mountains and hear the wolves howl at night. I gotta, Jess."

"If I find these men, I'm not plannin' to gun 'em down. I'll get 'em arrested and that's all."

"I'm not faultin' that. I just want free air."

"All right, Sam, but you write Ma and explain."

They stood for a long moment, listening to the distant singing of a night rider. The cattle were dog tired, Jess thought. There would be no trouble tonight.

"Darringer," Rocher said, appearing from the shadows.

Jess turned to look at the big, tall, hairy-faced man who looked older than his sixty-odd years. Rocher was all muscle and lean of belly, but he looked mighty tired.

"Jess, I'm right sorry for runnin' into your horse."

"We were all in a hurry," Jess said.

"I could have killed you. Listen, you take any of my horses."

"Thanks."

"I gotta tell you somethin'," the man added, his voice low, "and I ask you and your brother to tell no one else. It's my eyes, Jess. I just couldn't see what I was doin'. If anyone knew, I'd never get back on the trail. But I wanted you to know. Maybe you won't think so badly of me."

Jess swallowed, unsettled by the older man's troubles. "They won't hear it from us," he said.

They shook hands, and then Rocher wandered off into the darkness, leaving the Darringers touched and thoughtful. Jess sat on his heels, and Sam dropped down at his side.

A night rider was whistling. Jess knew nothing more pleasurable than riding night herd, sitting with his leg across the pommel of his Texas saddle, listening to the night wind, and singing a ballad to the longhorns under a starry sky.

He had left Sue Ellen for that kind of life, and now she was dead. For the first time, Jess had a twinge of loneliness. It was painful, and he was glad when Sam interrupted his thoughts.

"Looked like a mighty big herd out there," Sam said.

"We started with about a thousand cows and a couple of thousand steers. And fifteen men. We never lost a man, but I reckon we lost around a hundred head. And bargained a few to the Kiowa."

"After we find these men, will you let me head up the trail with you next spring?"

"I'd have to think on it. I'm a man that likes to ride alone."

Sam's eagerness was hard to resist. Jess stood up and stretched. It had been a long day, chasing the wild longhorns, and his saddle had nearly worn a hole in his Levi's. His legs were wobbly and sweat was thick in his clothes. He needed his rest now.

Reluctantly, Sam brought in his bedroll and plunked it down alongside Jess, but the older brother quickly rolled into his blankets. Feigning sleep, Jess turned on his side, but Sue Ellen's face continued to haunt him. He would have no peace until her killers were brought to justice. Only exhaustion put him to sleep.

In the morning, an hour before dawn, the cook was up and fanning the fire, and the smells of bacon and beans and strong coffee were filling the camp. Some of the men were stirring. Others had to be rousted out of their blankets. All were still weary from the previous day's ride.

Jess sat up and rubbed his shoulders. He turned, looking for Sam, and saw him already at the chuck wagon, filling his plate. It was just not going to be easy to keep up with his eager half brother.

It was another hard day of moving the cattle northwest on the rolling, treeless plain. They would be met by the big rancher who was building up his herd and breeding some of the longhorns with purebreds from the East.

Sam turned out to be one heck of a hand with his sorrel and the strays. He could spin his horse on a dime, and his rope was swift and sure. Jess was plenty proud of him.

"But it ain't much different from home," Sam complained.

It was a hot, dusty drive. Still worn from the stampede, the cattle dragged out for nearly a mile along the trail. Outriders met them and took over the herd by late afternoon, near a wandering creek. The foreman chatted with the owner, who drove up in a fancy buggy with a leather fringe. Count was taken, cash collected, and the men were paid off, handsomely.

Jess and his brother joined the others for a relaxing swim that also cleansed the sweat from their bodies. They were a group of white hides with brown faces and hands. Some wore their hats as they washed. Each had a good laugh at his companions.

Jess at last said farewell to his comrades, many of whom he would see again in the spring, and turned westward with Sam. The others headed east on the treeless plain, toward the nearest town and a hoot.

With Jess on his big bay and Sam on the sorrel, the Darringers were on the trail of men. Six-guns and rifles well oiled, they were going to seek justice.

They felt the increasing chill of night whenever they camped. At Sam's insistence, Jess often took his concertina from his pack and played and sang trail songs. The sweet tones of the instrument, like a small accordion, pleased them both. Jess had explained that his guitar was crushed when a stampede hurtled through camp. He had bought the squeezebox from a peddler, finding it easier to carry in its leather case.

One night Jess played "Green Grow the Lilacs," and after he finished, he enlightened Sam with a story.

"Seems like during the Mexican War, some

of our Irish soldiers kept singing that song. It was a real favorite. But the Mexicans who heard it, turned 'green grow' into 'gringo.' "

"You reckon that's true, Jess? I thought 'gringo' came from some Spanish word that meant foreigner."

"You've been going to school, have you?" Jess asked.

From then on they bantered back and forth on everything from the War Between the States to politics. It kept Jess from dwelling on their mission.

It took a week of traveling westward in the new state of Colorado just to be within sight of the Shining Mountains, the big Rockies. The only life they saw was a distant herd of fleeting white-tailed antelope and a circling turkey buzzard. At night they could hear the cry of the nighthawk and the lonely, eerie howl of the coyote. They were tired of their rations of bacon and beans. The biscuits were so hard that they had to soak them in coffee.

Sam told interesting stories of his two younger brothers, who were twins, and of his two sisters. Their mother, who now had credit for nine children, was also finding herself hostess to visiting nephews. The ranch was loaded with Darringers.

Sam's father, Jess' stepfather, sounded still as tough and unyielding as Jess remembered him. Sam talked also of his schooling. He was particularly enthusiastic about science, for he had an inquiring mind.

They camped their last night on the plains. It was cold, even by the fire. They were still burning buffalo and cow chips, which gave a pungent smell.

"Mighty lonesome country," Sam remarked. "Be glad to see some trees. Seems like we never get any closer to the mountains."

"You sure of the directions?"

"Sure. We just go west until we run into the main trail, then head north a day or so, then west again. Should be a sign. But it won't be any picnic. This fella we talked to, he said the Colbys are mighty tough and stick together. They run roughshod over everyone."

As Jess turned to roll up in his blankets, he wondered if a Colby really had been among the killers. Four or five brutal men had put their hands on sweet, sensitive, helpless Sue Ellen. Jess gritted his teeth and fought himself to sleep.

In the morning they broke camp and headed toward the red-streaked foothills of the Rockies. Beyond their view there were great mountains with white caps all year.

As they reached the new southbound tracks of the Denver and Rio Grande Railroad, Jess muttered his dislike of progress. The dark rails lay on timber in the turned sod, and they were like a long snake crossing the sea of brown grass.

When they struck the main trail that led north, they paused to read the signs. Tracks of wagons laden with ore or supplies, unshod Indian ponies, wobbling wheels from a settler's wagon, the thin tread of the local stage, sheep and cattle and horses—all crisscrossed in opposite directions.

"A lot of tales to tell here," Jess said.

They turned north alongside the beaten path, keeping off to the short grass between the rutted trail and the red, speckled foothills on their left.

Within hours they were trailing alongside great red boulders and scattered, stunted pines. The earth was red and often barren. To their right, the treeless plain rolled toward the flat, eastern horizon.

At one point they reined up as Jess surveyed westward tracks that were barely visible in the grass and red, choppy earth.

"Five horses cut off here," he said, "headin' pretty fast for them hills. One horse is lame. They dragged some brush over there where they hit dirt."

"You got a real good eye."

"Dust cloud," Jess said, straightening in the saddle.

They stayed off the main trail, resting their horses as they watched a group of some twenty riders approaching from the north. The riders slowed to a walk. They were carrying rifles and acting mighty mean. On a big roan, the graying and mustached leader looked as hard as nails, and he wore a badge. They halted some ten feet from the Darringers. Every horse in the posse was panting and dripping with sweat.

"You come up the trail?" the lawman asked, pushing his hat back from his wet brow. "I'm Marshal Clinton."

"We delivered a herd east of here, and are on our way to Buzzard's Creek," Jess responded politely.

"We just came from there. Express office was robbed. We figure it was some of the Hatchers what done it. What's your business in Buzzard's Creek?"

"We were plannin' to look at some land."

Clinton leaned forward on his pommel. His dark eyes narrowed as he took their measure.

"We're after four men. They grabbed one of the Colby women. We got no tracker, but we're bound to run 'em down."

"Jess can track 'em," Sam said.

"That so?"

Jess shrugged. He wasn't as sure a tracker as his brother Clay, but he was passable. Finally he nodded.

"I'd sure take it as a favor if you'd ride with us," Clinton said. "There's four of them and that poor woman."

"How long you been trailin'?" Jess asked.

"We ain't stopped since last night. They got an hour's start on us while we packed our saddles and mounted up."

"All right," Jess said, "but just you and me if you want that woman alive. Take a couple of mounts off your men and send the rest back."

"I'll stay too," Sam said.

"No," Jess countered. "You got things to do in Buzzard Creek."

The brothers stared at each other. Sam got the message that he could do a lot of poking around while waiting for Jess. Though a little disappointed, he nodded.

"You're right," Clinton said. "You men, two of you double up and give us your horses."

"Now, hold on," a young man told him, riding forward. "I'm the only Colby knows about this, and that's my sister out there."

"Take it easy, Neal," the lawman said.

Jess turned his steel gray eyes on Neal Colby, a man about Sam's age, blond, clean-shaven, and with a rather large nose and dark, wide-set eyes. He looked plenty mean and wore twin Colts.

Telling himself he had no proof that any Colby had murdered Sue Ellen, let alone this particular one, Jess still couldn't help grimacing. His gut was churning.

Clinton was carrying the conversation now,

and it was agreed that Jess, he, and Colby would be the only posse. The others turned back. Three men doubled up, leaving three weary horses.

Regretfully, Sam shook Jess's hand and rode northward, looking back with a forlorn wave.

"All right," Clinton said, "I figure we'll head on south. They're probably set for Mexico."

"First we rest those horses," Jess said, dismounting.

"Look, mister, whoever you are," Colby growled, "that's my sister they took. The longer we take, the less chance she's got. I don't want them slowin' down."

"You'll kill those horses," Jess said, loosening his cinch. "We got some shade in those cottonwoods."

The other men dismounted reluctantly. Jess led them down the trail, away from the signs he had found. Against the red boulders, shaded by two gnarled trees, they rested their horses and shared their canteens with them.

"They got to be halfway to Mexico," Neal Colby said, finally calming down enough to lean on a tree trunk.

Marshal Miles Clinton knew he was out of his jurisdiction, but that wasn't stopping him. Jess wondered if the Colbys paid him his wages.

"Now you know us," the lawman said. "So who are you, mister?"

"Jess Darringer."

"So you're one of them," Clinton said, looking him over.

Neal rested his hands on his Colts, studying Jess. Looking for danger, he found only an amiable cowhand. At least, that was the way Jess appeared. Yet the Darringers had a long reputation as gunfighters.

When the horses were rested, they cinched up and mounted. The lawman and Neal Colby headed quickly toward the trail, riding south, the extra horses following on a long catch rope fastened on Neal's saddle horn. The marshal was riding his roan while Neal had switched to a sorrel.

Calmly, Jess turned his mount back up the road. The others, surprised and agitated, came riding back to his side.

"What are you doing?" Neal demanded.

"Their trail is up here."

"You mean you knew all along where they was headed?" Neal snorted. "You dirty sidewinder!"

"It'll be dark in a few hours," the marshal said. "Neal's right. You should have told us."

"We got a better chance now," Jess responded. "I plan to stay alive. And if you want me to do the trackin', you'll ride a ways back and not disturb anything."

Neal leaned over from his saddle. "I don't see nothin'."

"Five horses," Jess said. "One of them is lame."

"All right, Darringer," Clinton said. "Lead on."

Jess sat quietly in the saddle, studying the boulders that barred most of the way into the western foothills. The giant red rocks looked like marbles in the green of the pines. Every little trail led to nowhere. The cliffs rising beyond the boulders were rugged and unfriendly.

Men could be there now, watching and waiting. It was a gamble.

Yet Jess, too, wanted to rescue the woman. He had to save her. And maybe it would ease his conscience for having left Sue Ellen on her own.

Overhead, a red-tailed hawk circled and screeched as it moved away, signaling trouble.

Slowly, Jess led the way, his big bay picking its path through the grass and rocks. A rifle could be aimed at him right now. At any moment, one of them might die.

Chapter Two

LEADING the way, Jess often stopped to dismount and kneel. Little rocks would be kicked from their sockets in the earth. Blades of grass would be crushed enough to stay bent. Lizard tracks were crossed. Signs of brush being dragged over barren ground were frequent.

Long shadows were after them now. There were more trees, stubby, bent, and gnarled. Some were scrub pine. Tall aspens lined what appeared to be a distant creek to the left. Brush still clung to the side canyons. Soft earth kept their movements quiet as they led their horses, although Jess was often annoyed by his companions' stumbling.

Occasionally, they had glimpses of the foothills and the blue streak of the great mountains beyond.

Neal Colby, his dark eyes glaring, grudgingly admitted that Jess knew what he was doing. The city marshal also could see that their only chance was with Jess's skill.

All three men knew that the great rocks ahead could be shielding a rifle. One or more of them could die at any moment.

"They're still ridin' scared," Jess said softly as they paused between the boulders. "The lame horse isn't going to make it. It has a loose shoe."

"That's my sister's mare," Neal muttered. "She was taking it to the smithy near the express office."

When they rounded the next turn, they found the woman's horse, its throat slit. The outlaws had rolled it down into a crevice. It had been a right pretty sorrel mare, its mane and tail groomed and fluffy. It had been dead for only an hour. Jess was surprised to see a Texas saddle on its back. The woman had been riding astride like a man. If she also had Neal Colby's large features, she couldn't be very attractive.

Their next find was one of the outlaws, a grimy-looking older man. Dead, with dry blood on his chest, he had been pulled into the shade with no protection from predators.

"I knew I hit one of 'em," the marshal said. "Maybe two, when they was trying to get out of town. He's a Hatcher all right. They're a dirty bunch."

It was near twilight when they found another man. Left wounded, he had died from loss of blood. Miles Clinton could claim them both. That left two men and the woman. And there wasn't going to be much of a moon.

"We can't track by night," Clinton said.

"We got to," Neal cut in. "I don't want them stoppin'."

"They're careless now," Jess said. "We can follow awhile longer, then look for their camp-fire, if they set one."

A pistol shot rang out from the rocks ahead and beyond. It wasn't aimed at them, and it echoed into the hills.

"You men stay back here," Jess muttered.

"Nothin' doin'," Neal said.

"You make more noise than a locomotive," Jess told him quietly. "Now, both of you stay put."

"He's right," Clinton said.

Dismounting to lead his horse, Jess left them behind. He was following a natural trail, confident that that was where they had ridden. The signs told him he was right.

It was nearly dark. The slice of moon wasn't giving much light. Soon he sniffed wood smoke. He left his horse ground-tied and moved on through the red-and-white-streaked boulders. There were no night birds. No scuffle of lizards. No call of a distant coyote. No breath of wind.

Another pistol shot rang out, and Jess moved faster, his six-gun in hand. The thieves were fighting over the loot, or the woman.

He spotted the campfire, hidden between the great rocks. It was smoldering, and next to it, facedown, lay a dead man, arms and legs sprawled. A side arm lay near his clutched right hand. There was blood on his back. He had been shot clean through.

Kneeling in the brush, Jess squinted, but he saw no one else.

"I'm gonna tear you apart," a man was shouting.

The voice came from up the little canyon to the right.

Another shot rang out. A rifle echoed. Then silence.

Taking a chance, Jess moved quickly into the opening between the walls of the canyon. As he rounded the bend and lost his footing, a shot whistled past his head, the report's echo bouncing along the walls.

Jess dived behind a pile of rocks on the right. Someone was holed up in the half-cave set in a ledge, high on the left wall. He would get around it by climbing and dropping from beyond. But first he had to cross that open space in the pale moonlight.

He paused, took a deep breath, then lunged across. Bullets whistled by his ear from behind him. He made it around the boulders on the left wall, and then kneeled out of sight. He saw another shot explode in the rocks on the right wall. He fired rapidly at the flash of moonlight on a man's face. There was a gasp and a crash into the brush.

Cautiously, Jess moved forward, his heart racing. There was sweat on his face. He could be walking into a bullet.

Easing his way through the rocks, he nearly stumbled on a man's body. In the pale light, he used his boot to roll the man over. He had shot him in the face. The man was dead.

This sight never pleased Jess. He hated to have to kill a man. It always left him shaken. He always whispered a prayer.

As he came back into the clearing, a rifle shot sang by his ear, and he dived for cover. It was either the woman or another Hatcher who might have met them here, someone who was a good shot, even in the dark.

Catching his breath, he moved far to his left, then began to climb up the steep incline. His left hand was bleeding when he got to the top. Wrapping his bandanna around it, he carefully made his way along the rim.

When he was past the cave and to its right, he slowly slid down the wall, ending up on the ledge that led to the hollow. Moving as silently as he could, he neared the opening.

There was a movement, and then a rifle appeared. Jess grabbed it, jerking it forward as he aimed his six-gun at the owner's gut. The rifle spun into the air and clattered down the wall. He grabbed a small arm, and was startled when he found himself staring at a wild-eyed young woman.

She stumbled onto the ledge, fighting fiercely to free her arm from his grasp. He couldn't let her go or she'd fall. Her long yellow hair flew about her face as she struggled. Pounding him wherever she could reach, she shoved his six-gun aside. Her long riding skirts and tight blue jacket were in the way of her every move.

Suddenly, in her hand, she held a long knife with a gleaming blade. She began to slash at him. He caught her wrist hard, and the knife went the way of the rifle. As they teetered on the edge, she kicked him in the right shin, brutally.

"I'm a friend," he managed to say, dodging her blows.

He holstered his gun and grabbed both her wrists, shaking her so hard that she gasped. Her dark eyes were wide-open, her lips trembling.

Only then did she pause, held tight by his big hands.

"I came with the marshal," he told her, catching his breath. "And your brother Neal."

"Oh, I'm sorry," she whispered, about to collapse.

He released her. Slowly she sank down, her hands to her chest. Jess kneeled at her side. Her hair fell forward and covered her face. She sobbed as she spoke:

"They got in a fight. While they were at it, I grabbed the rifle and ran. I heard a shot. Then one of them came after me. I thought I hit him, over on the far wall, in that brush. Then you came. I thought it was him."

"How many men were with you?"

"Four, but some had been shot."

"They're all gone now."

"Did *I* shoot him?"

"No, *I* did, before I came up to find you."

She seemed relieved, but was still stunned as she rose unsteadily. Abruptly, she started down the slope, slipping and sliding in the rocks. Jess hurried after her, afraid she would fall. He jumped several feet at a time, reaching the canyon floor ahead of her.

Then she lost her footing and came crashing down, her skirts and hair flying, rocks rolling under her feet. She cried out, but as she neared the bottom, Jess was there.

He caught her in midair, with his arm about her waist, and then set her down. Still holding her, fearful she would fall, he had a better look at her face.

She was in her early twenties and as pretty as a Texas sunrise. Her features were delicate and feminine. She gazed at him, her long lashes flickering. She was out of breath, and her lips parted as she tried to speak.

Jess was in no hurry to let her go. She smelled good, of lilac maybe. Her body was soft, yielding to the grip of his arm. He was trying to discover the color of her eyes when she closed them and fainted.

He swung her up into his arms. She didn't weigh much. Her head rested against his shoulder, her face covered by her silken hair. He carried her, his right leg sore from her kick.

Her long riding skirts swept the ground as he limped back through the canyon. Reaching the campfire, he set her down on some blankets. As her head rolled back, her hair spread in a silken sweep around her. She was as small and fragile as Sue Ellen.

After dragging the other body over and down into a ditch, he returned to kneel at the fire, stoking it up and letting the bright flames cast a glow on her peach-colored skin.

Then Jess went back into the canyon to recover the rifle she had been using. He dragged the body of the fourth man to the canyon opening, so that it would be easier to find in the morning.

He returned to the campfire weary, and uneasy at being alone with this young, all too lovely woman. Taking the rifle in hand, he fired three shots. They echoed in the night, vibrating off the great boulders.

The woman gasped and rose on her elbow. She stared up at Jess, slowly recognizing him as her rescuer. Now she was blushing, beautifully. Her voice was as soft as the wind, and her dark eyes were shy as she said, "I've never fainted in my life."

"You earned the right."

"Who are you?"

"Jess Darringer."

"You're one of those gunfighters?"

"Well, ma'am, mostly I've been ridin' trail. We just delivered a herd southeast of here, up from Texas."

"I'm Lorena Colby," she said, sitting up.

They paused as they heard horses crashing through the brush. It sounded like an army, but it was only the marshal and her brother. They reined up among the boulders, near Jess's bay, dismounted, and moved forward along the trail.

Neal hurried to kneel by his sister. He took her hand and grinned with delight.

"You gave us a scare," he said.

"They didn't hurt me," she responded.

Neal helped her pull the blankets up around her. The night was cold and crisp, the fire hot and crackling.

After unsaddling the horses and watering them in a nearby stream, they rested. Tomorrow, the Hatcher men would have to be buried or taken back. They managed to make a meal out of some beans and jerky that the outlaws had left behind. The marshal collected the loot, stuffed in four saddlebags. He took time to count it out. Then he told Lorena, "Jess here is the tracker who brought us on your trail. If it wasn't for him, we'd have been halfway to Mexico."

She lay back, drawing her blankets around her, and gazed up at Jess. He was still trying to see the color of her eyes. Blue, maybe. Whatever the color, they were shining in the starlight. With a faint smile, after gazing at him a while, she slowly closed her eyes. He tried not to look at her as she slept on her side, blankets drawn about her, golden hair near her face and throat.

"She's lucky we run into you," Clinton said.

"The Colbys are obliged," Neal added. "We'll be showin' our gratitude. A Colby never forgets a favor."

"No need," Jess said.

"Ed Grange will be thanking you as well," Clinton said. "He's planning to marry her, and he'll be mighty grateful."

"He's a clod," Neal snarled.

Jess was interested in this strong reaction, but it was soon explained by Clinton.

"Neal here takes exception to competition. Lorena isn't really his sister. She was an orphan. They raised her like a Colby."

"Don't be tellin' our business," Neal said grumpily.

Jess understood now why Lorena was so

lovely and Neal so homely. He wondered why a family apparently so tough and power hungry would bother to take in a foundling.

"Ed Grange works for the railroad," Clinton said. "He has a lot to say about whether a spur comes west to Buzzard's Creek. I reckon everyone wants the railroad except the freighters and stage line."

"And me," Neal growled. "I like things the way they are."

"Your family could ship their gold and cattle right from town," the lawman reminded him. "The place will grow plenty big, and your family owns most of it."

"The railroad brings in farmers," Neal said.

"You have all the hill country north of town and the mesa besides. You got more land than a man can ride in one direction in half his lifetime. The farmers and small ranchers are mostly down on the flats."

Neal grunted. "Next thing you know, the sheep will come. And barbed wire."

"You can't stop it," Clinton said.

Neal growled, then downed his coffee, lay down, and rolled in his blankets. When he was snoring, Clinton turned to Jess with more information.

"Lorena was five when her Pa discovered a gold deposit up in the canyon. Mighty rich ore. But the Cheyenne swept through and killed her folks. Lance Colby found her hidin' in the creek, and the Colbys took her in, along with the mine. Then came the gold rush and they got rich. Lance raised her like family, even signed over a share of the ranch when she turned eighteen. She was never adopted, but she's a Colby."

"They got rich from her mine?" Jess asked.

"Partly, but they built the first buildings in town, right on their land, north side of the creek. Now they got shares in nearly everything. Gave a lot of grubstakes. Lent a lot of money. And collected. What's built up on the south side of the creek, they got no say about."

Jess leaned back on his elbow, staring into the leaping flames. Beyond the fire it was cold and dark, but here the warmth and glow were mighty comfortable. He had missed the smell of wood smoke for a long time.

He glanced over at Lorena Colby, her face hidden by the blanket. Neal was still snoring quietly, his belly rising up and down.

"What about this Ed Grange?" he asked Clinton.

"Strange fella. I seen him target practicin' down by the creek. Mighty fast draw for a railroad man."

"Where do you fit in?"

"For a Texan, you ask an awful lot of questions."

They studied each other a while. Then Clinton shrugged. When he answered, his voice was lower:

"Well, for a lawman, I'm gettin' mighty old. When the Colbys voted me in, I figured I was gonna retire right there. But things are buildin' up. There's the Hatcher bunch south of town and they're breedin' like rabbits. They won't be thankin' us for this day's work. There's going to be trouble, but knowin' them, they'll take their time and hit us when we don't expect it."

"What about the Colbys? Big family?"

"Old man Colby had seven sons by his first two wives. Widowed twice. His third wife is trying to make a lady out of Lorena. His other sons have married and sprouted kids, but Neal's stayed single."

"Any of them been down in Texas lately?"

The marshal shook his head as if he didn't know. He looked at the sleeping Colbys, became a little nervous about the conversation, and he cut it off suddenly. Jess would get no more information.

"And what about you?" Clinton asked as he rolled out his blankets. "I hear you Darringers are nothin' but gunfighters. In fact, your brother Ben outdrew and gunned down the Texas Killer last spring, over in Arizona."

"Ben's a lawyer now."

"Mighty fast switch. And you?"

"Been on the cattle trail four years. Saving up to buy me a spread."

Clinton glanced at Jess's side arm, and then stretched out and rolled into his blankets.

Jess poked at the fire with a stick. Wood sure smelled a lot better than the chips they had been burning on the trail. When Clinton was breathing heavily, Lorena sat up.

"I've been listening," she said.

"Didn't mean to keep you awake."

"You're awfully curious about the Colbys."

"I might settle in this country. Man likes to know who his enemies might be."

She frowned at him and drew her blankets more tightly about her. Her dark blue eyes, the color of a mountain lake, glistened in the firelight. Her shimmering hair fell about her face and shoulders. Her voice was soft and low.

"I'm beholden to you for finding me," she said. "But I have to warn you, Mr. Darringer. Stay away from my family."

Her delicate features were shadowed by the fire. He noticed for the first time that she had a slight bump on the bridge of her pretty nose. It made her all the more interesting.

"Didn't mean to alarm you," he said. "I'm looking for some men who killed a woman down in Texas last July. I'd be obliged if you kept that to yourself."

Startled by his trust, she lay back on her

elbow. He had confused her. She studied him a while before asking, "Did you know her?"

He nodded. Suddenly tongue-tied, he poured himself some more coffee as he watched her retreat into her blankets.

On the first watch, he could only sit and remember Texas, but he often glanced at the spun-gold hair spread across Lorena's face and throat as she slept.

In the morning, Lorena prepared breakfast and made very good coffee. The sun had trouble reaching them through the rocks and trees. The men loaded the first two Hatchers, rolled in blankets, on two of the spare horses. The outlaws' mounts had run off during the fight.

Jess couldn't help watching Lorena move around the camp. She was graceful, gentle, and quiet. Even if she was a Colby, he was glad she was safe. He might think of her now and then when he was wandering the prairie after this was over.

"There's going to be trouble," Clinton said as they saddled up. "The Hatchers aren't going to take kindly to losin' four of 'em."

"They'd just better hang back," Neal growled. "We've been lookin' for an excuse to clean 'em out."

On the path east, they picked up one of the Hatcher horses. Loading another body on it, and the fourth on their other spare horse, they headed for the main trail.

As they continued riding through the rocks, Jess took the lead. Often he found himself looking back at Lorena. She sat the horse like a cowhand, riding astride with her every movement tied in with the animal's. She was hatless, her hair blowing in the slight wind. She looked beautiful.

When they reached the main trail and headed north, it was already late afternoon. Buzzards were circling. The men had to choose between riding late at night into town and camping along the trail with four bodies.

All the horses except Jess's were bone weary. They reluctantly made camp as evening fell, settling deep in the trees and rocks, trying to conceal their campfire.

"Still a few Cheyenne raidin'," Clinton told Jess. "They're a mean-tempered bunch and won't forget the bad hands we dealt 'em."

"They dealt Custer one of their own," Jess reminded him.

"I ain't afraid," Neal bragged. "I'd like to run into 'em. Give me some target practice."

"I'm not sure we'd enjoy it," Clinton said dryly.

As they huddled around the fire, the cold night circling them, Clinton called attention to Jess's squeezbox, but Jess declined to play, too embarrassed in front of Lorena. Besides, she looked exhausted from her ordeal.

Neal Colby was soon rolled up in his blankets, snoring softly. While Jess and Clinton talked about the War Between the States, Lorena also curled up and fell asleep.

It was then, yearning for a song, that Jess took up his squeezebox, his prized concertina. He'd been told that he had a good singing voice, but either way it wouldn't matter to the marshal. Most of the songs he knew were trail songs.

Waiting until he was certain that the Colbys were sound asleep, he crossed his legs and moved back from the fire, unable to stop the music his deft hands had chosen.

The sweet refrain of "Red River Valley" moved with his fingers. His voice, low and soft, brought forth the plaintive words:

> "Come and sit by my side if you love
>   me,
> Do not hasten to bid me adieu,
> But remember the Red River Valley
> And the cowboy who loved you so
>   true."

He could sing no more, but continued playing, the words ringing in his heart as he thought of Sue Ellen. Finally it was too much for him, and he set the squeezebox aside, offering to take the first watch, not looking at the lawman. He didn't want him to see his pain.

As Clinton rolled up in his blankets, Jess turned to look at Lorena. The firelight was aglow on her face. Her eyes were open and glistening.

Embarrassed, Jess took up his rifle and walked out of the firelight to find a spot among the rocks. He drew his leather coat more tightly about him. It was mighty cold away from camp.

Now that he had slipped the word to Lorena about his search for the killers, all of the Colbys would be on their guard. They sounded too arrogant to bother hiding the locket or music box. His plan had to be to keep pushing and prodding.

The one way to ease his pain from the news of Sue Ellen's murder was to track down the killers, even if it meant a bullet in his back.

Chapter Three

IN the morning, Jess avoided Lorena as she prepared breakfast. He was shy around women, and he was sorry she had heard him sing. He grinned as he realized that *she* might also be sorry.

They finally broke camp. Loading the outlaws on the spare horses, Neal grumbled again about the south hills being wasted on the Hatchers.

"They got heaps of grass," he said. "Hardly any cattle. And I been wondering where they get all their loot."

"We have the men that robbed the express office, and we got the money back," Clinton said. "That's all we have to be concerned about."

"We got nearly ten thousand head of cattle to feed, and the Hatchers ain't usin' their grass."

"You got plenty of grass, and there's hundreds of miles of open range east of here," Clinton countered.

"And some of the big ranchers out there are havin' their men file homestead papers to tie up the range," Neal reminded him.

Clinton shrugged as he turned to saddle his own horse.

Back on the main trail north, they rode a few hours before coming to a fork in the road. A wooden sign had *Buzzard's Creek* carved on it, and an arrow pointing west. As they rode in the town's direction, deep into the foothills, they soon crossed the waters of Buzzard's Creek. At this point, some five miles east of town, it was spread sixty feet wide and was only four to five feet deep. More like a river than a creek, the water was swift and clean, headed for the flats. The horses easily forded it to the north bank.

"Best water this side of the Rockies," Neal said.

They watered the horses and rested in the shade of tall, stately, shimmering aspens. The stream was ice cold from the mountains. Jess filled his canteen even though they were close to town, because a man never knew when he'd have to ride. His main concern now, however, was that his bay was favoring its right foreleg because the sole of the hoof had been slightly bruised by the rocks.

They remounted and started westward

again, with Jess riding his horse in the soft dirt and grass. The sunlight was strong and warm, as it was already noon. The foothills ahead were hidden by the great stacks of red rocks and stumpy trees.

Soon they were in the open and in sight of the town. On both sides were rolling and grassy hills, steep and barely wooded. On the south side, mines dotted the heights.

The buildings faced the streets on both sides of the creek, which disappeared westward into a steep rocky canyon. Above the ridges, beyond the mesa, the Rocky Mountains lay in a mist of blue and white. Jess smiled. Sam must have loved his first sight of them.

As they drew near the town on the north side of the creek, Jess could see that on his left, the southern side, across the wooden bridge, there were mostly saloons and freight offices, all facing the street and water. An ore smelter was set back on a knoll, not far from the local boot hill.

"Hatcher country," Neal said.

On the northern side, the livery, blacksmith, express office, newspaper, jail, hotel, stores, and one saloon were situated in a row in that order, all facing the street and water. Up on a knoll behind the livery were a little white church and a cemetery. Farther along, also on a knoll, was a little red schoolhouse. Beyond that, homes dotted the hillside or were set behind the stores.

Wagons, horses, and mules were everywhere, with farmers, ranchers, and merchants all mingling. Several children were playing with a little white dog. A group of women were leaving the express office.

As they entered the main street on the north side, Jess glanced south across the creek. Next to an old, leaning hotel there was a gunsmith and Morley's saddlery.

He concentrated now on the crowds gathering on the boardwalk on the north side near the express office. Watching for Sam, he let his bay draw away from the parade.

Lorena and Neal led the cavalcade. The marshal followed with the Hatchers thrown across the saddles. Men came forward to help. Jess reined up by the livery while the others continued up the street. He dismounted and led his bay through the big, open doors. A few men were lounging about; others were asleep. It was dusty, the back doors open to the breeze. Horses were lined up in stalls on either side and in the back corrals. Jess turned to the old gent who was chewing on a pipe and walking toward him. Bearded, bald, and basically unclean, the man appeared friendly.

"My name's Potter. This here's my place."

"Need a stall."

"I got an old one at the end, but it's open to the wind."

Jess accepted it, paid the man, and put up his horse. After leaving his gear with Potter, he turned back into the street. All the excitement was up at the jail. He just wasn't interested. Until Sam appeared from the blacksmith's.

They shook hands and started slowly up the boardwalk. Sam had already heard about the four Hatchers. Jess filled him in on his experience with the marshal, Lorena, and Neal. He told Sam that he had mentioned to Lorena that they were looking for men who had killed a woman in Texas, but he had asked her not to tell anyone.

"We'll see if any Colbys start sweatin'," Jess said.

"What if she doesn't repeat what you said?"

"That ain't likely. She was an orphan. They took both her and her father's mine, and raised her like a Colby. She's plenty loyal to 'em."

"Well, I learned that the Colbys hate the Hatchers, and there are some Hatchers in the saloons across the creek." Sam nodded across the wooden bridge that was maybe ten feet wide and twenty feet long. "This bein' Saturday, there might be trouble tonight, because there are some Colbys in the saloon on this side of the creek."

"You been over to Morley's?"

"Yeah, I talked to the old fella there. He says he makes all receipts for even dollars. He has no idea when any receipt was written. He has a lot of business from the Colbys and everyone else. Most often, he hands out his work without collecting the receipts. I paid him to forget I asked, but I didn't see he had any loyalty to anyone except his wallet. Anyway, we need more than that piece of paper, Jess."

"It gave us a name."

"There are an awful lot of Colbys. Lance Colby and seven sons, plus, I'd say, thirty or forty family members. And that many hired hands, or more."

"Lorena Colby's set to marry a railroad man, an Ed Grange. Is he around?"

"Yeah, and so is his sister," Sam said, nodding up the street.

Leaving the newspaper office was a young woman in her early twenties, wearing a frilly blue dress with a white shawl. She had dark brown hair and eyes, nice features, and a sweet smile that she threw their way. Both men quickly tipped their hats.

"Miss Elizabeth Grange," Sam said, "may I present my brother Jess Darringer?"

"The tracker," she said. "I've just heard."

"We're about to go to the hotel for something to eat," Sam said. "You're welcome to join us."

"That would be naughty," she responded, smiling, "and I'd love to, but I'm not allowed."

"Is your brother in town?" Jess asked.

"He's at the hotel. Do you know him?"

"No."

"You're going to ask to call on me?" she inquired.

Startled, Jess could only stare at her. She had him at a decided disadvantage. Her flirtation was unexpected. He didn't know what to do, so he just stood dumbfounded.

Moving past them toward the express office, she gave Jess a smile he would not soon forget.

As they walked on, Sam grinned at his half brother. "Now you have two women on your hands."

"How do you figure that?"

"Well, Lorena Colby's been tellin' everybody how you saved her. Sounds to me like she was impressed."

"That sort of thing wears off."

As they walked, Jess tugged his wide-brimmed Stetson lower on his brow to avoid the sun. He studied the town on both sides of the creek. He was marking detail, just in case. A man never knew when he would need cover.

The buildings on either side needed fresh paint. They were weather-beaten and tired, and some of them were leaning. The people in the street on the north side, the church side, were better dressed. Wagons were being filled with trade goods. On the south side, horses lined the railings in front of the many saloons.

Sam and Jess walked around the noisy crowd outside the jail. They could hear Neal's loud voice:

"One of these days, those Hatchers gotta go. I'll bet they're behind every rustlin' we've had."

Jess shook his head, glad to be away from the noise. He was hungry and tired. Being around women plumb wore him out.

"I got us a room at the hotel," Sam was saying. "The barber's on the other side of it. You can get a hot bath there."

As they neared the large frame hotel with its full balcony and wide porch, Jess paused. Lorena was standing near the top step with an older, gray-haired woman in a green silk dress, a woman who was obviously protective of Lorena.

"Mr. Darringer," Lorena called.

Sam and Jess hesitated, but then moved onto the lower porch steps and tipped their hats. Lorena's golden hair was glistening in the sunlight. During the introductions they learned that the older woman was her foster mother.

"You'll have to excuse my daughter," Mrs. Colby said. "She needs her rest."

"I didn't have a chance to thank you," Lorena said to Jess.

"We all thank you," her mother said. "My

husband will thank you properly. Come along, Lorena. The wagon's waiting. We want to be home before dark."

Lorena cast a shy glance toward the Darringers as she followed her mother up the street. Sam told Jess, "I get the feeling that no man's going to get near Lorena Colby, unless he's got money like that Ed Grange."

"Let's get that bath and shave," Jess said, rubbing his whiskers as he watched the women climb onto a buckboard driven by an old cowhand. As she rode from town, Lorena turned and looked back.

"Wish women would look at *me* like that," Sam mused.

"Your time will come, and then you'll be mighty sorry."

The barber shop, tucked between the hotel and a general store, was small but not too messy. A bald little man gave them shaves and collar-length haircuts before sending them to the back room for Jess's bath. Sam helped by pouring hot water over Jess as he sank lower in the big iron tub. The room was cold, with steam rising. Closing his eyes, Jess enjoyed the hot water and comfort.

"You really don't like women much, do you, Jess?"

"They scare me plenty."

"You ain't never gettin' married?"

"Not a chance," Jess said, sinking deep.

"You mean if Lorena Colby asked you, it'd be no?"

"You're just whistling 'Dixie,'" Jess grunted. "No use even thinkin' about somethin' that ridiculous."

Jess sank deeper in the water, refusing to entertain such a fantasy. It was the best defense he could muster.

After Jess was dry and dressed, he felt more human, and he pulled on his Stetson and walked with Sam back into the street. It was late afternoon. They went to a store where Jess got new, stiff Levi's and a clean blue, double-breasted shirt. He changed into them, and with his leather jacket thrown over his arm, they returned to the street.

It was near dark. Across the creek, the lights were blazing, and they could hear the music from an old piano. There was a lot of shouting. Someone fired off a pistol, twice. Then there was laughter.

"The Hatchers and some of the miners," Sam suggested.

They entered the hotel and found its lobby large and empty. The clerk was away from his desk. The furniture was green and white and soft. The drapes around the great windows were emerald green with a long fringe. Fancy brass lanterns burned low around the room.

"Dining room's out back," Sam told Jess, leading the way.

The lamps were brighter here, and the room was large. There was one long center table where six men were seated. Many smaller tables lined the walls and were spread across the room.

Jess and Sam seated themselves at a table by the back wall. A stooped, elderly waiter came over to take their order for steak and potatoes.

"That's Grange there," Sam said quietly. "Sittin' at the head of the table, facin' us."

Jess studied the man, who was apparently in his forties. He was tall and husky but homely, with a hard face and a tight mouth. His mustache was thin and black like his hair. His eyes were a light blue. He wore a fancy blue velvet vest under his dark suit.

Jess took an immediate dislike to him and decided that the Colbys were sacrificing Lorena to the railroad. She was so loyal that she would do as they asked. Maybe he was mistaken, but the very thought of such a bargain riled Jess. His face tightened into a grimace.

"What's wrong?" Sam murmured.

"I don't like his looks," Jess said.

Sam grinned as if he figured that Jess had fallen for Lorena, but that wasn't it at all, as far as Jess was concerned. She was lovely and young. This man was harsh and uncompromising.

"One thing I know how to do," Jess said,

"and that's read men. They're like a trail in the mud, easy to figure."

While they ate their dinner, the men at the long table began to laugh. Grange was in charge. The others seemed to be local merchants and ranchers who were seeking favors from the big man.

"To the railroad," Grange said, lifting his glass.

The others followed suit: "To the railroad!"

As Elizabeth Grange entered the dining room, the men at the long table stood up to greet her and invite her to join them. She cast a flirtatious glance at Jess.

"You know," Sam said, his voice low, "I just figured out why women like you. You don't want them. That's a real challenge."

"I reckon."

Jess savored his steak. "On the trail," he said, "you don't eat your own beef. Maybe a buffalo now and then, or someone else's stray. And sometimes, especially after a stampede when you get separated from the chuck wagon, you don't eat at all."

It was then that the marshal and another man entered the dining room. Looking like a rancher, the second man had a brown leather vest over his woolen shirt. His hat was off, showing his sandy, thinning hair. His face was lined and hard, with a strong nose and narrow brown eyes under heavy brows. He wasn't a big man, but he looked plenty tough.

The two men walked past the long table where the Granges were sitting and stopped next to Sam and Jess.

"Jess Darringer," Clinton said, "I want you to meet Lance Colby."

"I wanted to thank the man who helped save my daughter," the rancher said.

"This is my brother Sam," Jess responded as he shook hands with the man.

Colby's grip was firm, his face crinkled and friendly. The marshal left, and the rancher pulled up a chair, accepting coffee from the waiter.

"I'll be payin' for your suppers," Colby said.

"Not necessary," Jess replied.

"Son, you're in Colby country. Sooner or later you're gonna find out no one argues with me."

Jess grinned. He couldn't help but like him.

Ed Grange left his table to come over and stand by Colby's chair. He shook hands with the rancher, who introduced them to the Darringers.

"Mr. Colby," Grange said, "I'd be obliged if you would join us at our table."

"Not right now," Colby growled. "Can't you see I'm busy with my new friends?"

"Well, when you have time," Grange said, annoyed.

Colby watched him go back to his table, then leaned forward and spoke in a low voice.

"He's got somethin' I want for this town, but it don't mean I gotta like him."

"But he's gonna marry your daughter," Sam blurted out.

"That ain't for sure," Colby said.

Jess thought this over. It appeared that Lorena was the carrot dangling in front of the donkey. Colby had to be one tough man to do business with.

"I hear you fellas are from Texas," the rancher said. "I figure you're both pretty good hands. Are you lookin' for work?"

"Could be," Jess told him. "But my horse is lame. I gotta rest him awhile."

"You take your pick of my stock," Colby offered. "Any horse you see on my ranch, it's yours to own."

That offer appealed to Jess, and he leaned forward.

"Besides," Colby went on, "I wasn't thinkin' about just herdin' cattle. I was figurin' on the Darringer reputation."

"Why would you want to be hirin' gun hands?" Sam asked.

"Well, son, we got this feud goin' with the Hatchers. For a long time, they just stayed back in them south hills where they belonged, comin' to town for grub and a few drinks. But they busted out when they came and robbed the express office. And I ain't forgettin' how they grabbed my daughter while I was off at the ranch."

"So what are you planning?" Jess asked.

"We've been losin' a lot of cattle. I figure it's the Hatchers, but I ain't caught 'em. My men ain't gunfighters or trackers."

"It's not my line of work," Jess said. "I've spent most of my time on the cattle trail."

"But you were in that range war in Arizona with your brothers. The marshal's heard plenty about you Darringers."

"Jess," Sam said, "we could run out of money sleeping in this hotel and eatin' here."

"What are the wages?" Jess asked.

"I'll pay thirty a month and board."

"Not enough," Jess told him.

Colby leaned back in his chair, studying Jess's stern face. Then he grinned, showing crooked teeth.

"You're right," the rancher said. "Forty."

"Fifty," Jess said. "And we don't shoot unless we're shot at. And we take our orders direct from you, not your foreman or ramrod."

"All right, son. When can you fellas start?"

"Monday."

"Why not tomorrow?" the rancher asked.

"That's Sunday. I plan to go to church."

Colby considered this as he looked Jess and Sam over carefully. It was obvious that they were a new breed of gunfighter to him.

"Done," he said, and shook their hands.

Colby gave the waiter money for the steaks. Then he stood up and walked over to the long table, where he joined the Grange party.

"Well," Sam said, "that's one way to get close to the Colbys. It'll be easier to smell them out."

"Or get shot in the back," Jess said.

They finished their meal and stood up. As they walked past the long table, Grange cast a suspicious look at them, but his sister was smiling at Jess, her dark eyes twinkling. Any man who courted her would have his hands full, Jess thought, trying hard not to be interested.

Upon the dark street, lights from windows were tracing lines on the boardwalk. It was quiet on this side of the creek, but they could hear the saloon noise on the other side.

"Want to take a look?" Jess asked.

"We're here to find a Colby, and it's dangerous to go over there."

"Seems we oughta meet up with the Hatchers since we're likely gonna be exchangin' lead with 'em."

"You know, Jess, I get the feelin' you aren't as peaceable as you let on."

Jess grinned, and the two brothers, knowing that they were asking for trouble, started walking toward the bridge.

Chapter Four

As they crossed the bridge from north to south, Jess and Sam both felt the sudden tension.

The plank bridge was about ten feet wide and twenty feet long, with a four-foot railing. Water swirled below in a deep chasm as it sped onward, carrying the chill of the mountains. Jess liked the sound of racing streams, and he paused to look down at the way it glistened in the moonlight.

Facing the bridge was the freight office. To their left were the miners' supply stores, the saddlery, a gunsmith, and an old shanty of a hotel. To their right were five saloons, lined up in a row, some loud with music and laughter.

Beyond the saloons, the hills rose up in a sweep of little lights where mines were marked and being worked. Some were right at the entrance to the steep canyon of Buzzard's Creek.

"I'm not so sure this is a good idea," Sam said.

"Just because one of them killers had a Colby receipt, it don't mean it wasn't stolen from a Colby. In fact, those killers could have been Hatchers."

"Still, I feel like we're a pair of rabbits wandering into a wolf pack."

They walked across the rutted dirt street and onto the boardwalk, moving westward. Their boots made clicking sounds. The night was cold, the air still. Stars and a quarter moon were above in the black sky. Jess felt hemmed in by the hills and town. He would rather be riding the range than be here on a manhunt. He glanced at Sam, young and full of fire.

"Did you write Ma what you were doin'?"

"Mailed it this morning when the stage was leavin'."

"Anything happens to you, she'll have my hide."

Sam grinned, but he sobered as they stopped near the first saloon and looked in through the smoky window. This wasn't a lively place. Several miners were playing cards. The barkeep was carrying on an argument with some men at the bar. A drunk was asleep in the corner. There were no women.

Moving on to the second saloon, they again looked in the window. It was more crowded, but the men looked like miners. They were grubby and dirty, hardly any of them armed, and none of them was spoiling for a fight. Most were drinking or playing cards. Again, there were no women. Mules were tied out front.

At the third saloon, they paused again. Music and laughter were coming forth. The horses at the railing looked like cow ponies. Looking in the window, they saw a few miners and no women. The rest of the crowd were cowhands, all wearing side arms.

"Hatchers," Sam said. "That old one at the front table, he's called Bull. Head of the clan."

Jess studied him through the dirty window. Bull was big-shouldered and powerful, even in his declining years. He had a full head of wiry brown hair and a heavy beard. His hat was pushed back as he dealt the cards.

"All six around his table are his sons," Sam added.

Jess studied them. They looked a little wild, but no more so than most cowhands out for a Saturday night. One fellow was raising a fuss about his cards. He was in his twenties, red-faced and beady-eyed. His brothers were laughing at him, making him all the more irritated.

In the left corner, a round man at the piano was playing a lively tune. He had a cigarette dangling from his lip. Other men sat at tables and played cards. At the bar, an old man was talking with the bald bartender.

The Darringers turned and entered through the swinging doors. Only the Hatchers seemed to notice them. To Jess's right, the old man at the bar was busy with his bottle.

Jess leaned on the solid walnut rim of the bar. There was a huge, ornate glass mirror on the wall behind it. The bald and disgruntled bartender came to take their order.

"What's in that jug back there?" Jess asked.

"Cider."

"That's what we'll have."

As the smirking bartender poured their drinks, Jess and Sam looked into the huge mirror. They could see the Hatchers watching them.

The old man at the bar near Jess was chewing tobacco. He spat into the spittoon near Jess's boot, but was ignored. Finally, the red-faced Hatcher shoved his chair back, stood up, and swaggered over to them. His red woolen shirt was torn at the pocket, and around his neck was a checkered bandanna. He leaned on the bar between Jess and the old man.

"You fellas strangers around here?"

"Just got in," Jess said.

"I'm Red Hatcher. And there are only two sides around here, Hatchers or Colbys."

Jess took a swig of his cider, not answering.

"Hey, mister, I'm talkin' to you," Hatcher said.

"You haven't said much," Jess responded.

Hatcher's fist suddenly knocked the glass from Jess's hand. It flew into the glasses on the back counter, shattering everything it touched. The barkeep ducked, and the room went silent.

Slowly, Jess turned to look at Hatcher. "Somethin' wrong with you?" he asked.

Fuming, Hatcher stood spread-legged, his hand dangling near his six-gun. Jess ignored him and nodded to the bartender to bring another glass.

"Mister, you're really askin' for it," Hatcher said. "I'm figurin' you for a Colby man."

"He's Jess Darringer," Sam said from behind Jess.

The silence was heavy. Jess could hear his own breathing. He knew that Sam was getting nervous.

Red Hatcher stiffened slightly, then slowly began to smile, a sneer that twisted his red face. "So Colby brought in some hired guns," he snarled.

Standing but four feet from Jess, the man could hardly contain himself, his fingers opening and closing next to his holster. "Well," Hatcher continued, "I'm not afraid of you."

The barkeep delivered another glass of cider to Jess, and Hatcher snickered, then laughed.

"So that's all there is to a Darringer," he snorted. "Sweet apple cider."

Jess sipped his drink, ignoring him. But from the corner of his eye, he saw Hatcher's right hand make its move.

Spinning about and reaching, Jess slammed

his right fist into the man's face. The jerked-up six-gun fired into the ceiling even as Jess's left hand tore it from Hatcher's grasp.

Hatcher went flying backward, stunned. He crashed against the old man, then staggered and fell flat on his rear. He sat spraddle-legged, staring at Jess. It had happened so fast that he hadn't had time to breathe.

His six-gun in Jess's hand, Hatcher slowly regained his senses. His pride and dignity shattered, he considered how he looked, sitting on his rear on the saloon floor. Anger turned to fury, and he scrambled to his feet. Unsteady, touching the blood on his mouth, he glared at Jess as he planned his next move.

Jess looked down at the spittoon near his boot. He dropped in Hatcher's six-gun, barrel first. Then he looked at the man's face, which was turning redder by the second.

"You're a dead man, Darringer!" Hatcher snarled.

Jess turned and sipped his drink, gazing into the mirror. He could see Bull Hatcher and the others watching. Any minute now, they'd be coming at him and Sam.

He saw Sam all tight and ready, standing at his left side. Casually, he ordered another glass of cider and tossed coins on the bar.

Red Hatcher retrieved his gun, dripping with tobacco juice. Uncertain if it would fire safely, he hesitated, then turned and stormed back to his table. The silence in the saloon was deadly.

Slowly, Jess turned and looked around the room. All eyes were on him. With practiced calm, he pulled his hat down tight and started walking toward the swinging doors, Sam following some ten feet behind.

Pausing near Bull Hatcher, Jess looked down into the meanest pair of dark eyes he'd ever seen. The old man's beard was twitching with his tightening jaw.

"Howdy," Jess said.

Then he moved out the swinging doors, Sam following.

He continued down the sidewalk and back toward the bridge. Sam kept looking back nervously.

"They'll come after us," Sam said.

"Not tonight."

"How can you be so sure?"

"We took 'em by surprise."

"You sure did. That was the darnedest thing I ever saw."

"You won't tell Ma, will you?"

Sam looked at Jess's grin and had to laugh, but all the way to the bridge he kept looking back. No one was following.

"What made you take 'em on like that?" Sam asked.

"Learned it from the Comanche. You attack

an overpowering enemy in a show of bravado, and it throws 'em for a loop."

"Well, you sure made a couple of enemies," Sam said.

"That's what Colby wants."

"But what good will it do us?"

"It'll put the Colbys at ease. They'll talk too much."

They reached the bridge and crossed, heels clunking loudly on the planks. They walked over the rutted dirt street to the boardwalk in front of the newspaper office, and then turned right to the livery where they would pick up Jess's gear.

This side of the creek, the town was quiet. Lights were aglow from the single saloon at the end of the street. It was Saturday night on the south side, not here.

"I'll bet that when the Colby riders cross over, there's one heck of a brawl," Sam remarked.

Jess checked his bay. It wasn't lame, just sore-footed and in need of a lot of rest. He'd have it reshod in a month.

After picking up Jess's gear, they returned to the street and headed for the hotel. Once again the lobby was empty. They walked up the winding stairs, with their green carpet and shining, walnut bannister. When they reached the landing, Sam led the way to a front room that overlooked the street.

The tall, narrow window had dirty white curtains. There were two chairs, a dresser, and a bed with a heavy pile of blankets. A green rug lay on the wooden floor.

"Well," Jess said, sitting on the wide bed, "we got one night of comfort. Then it's the bunkhouse."

"We really goin' to church tomorrow?"

"Ma would like it."

Sam shrugged, agreeing, but still looking for all that excitement he had been seeking away from home.

"That was some fight," Sam said, sitting down in a horn chair to pull off his boots. "If you can draw as fast as you moved your fist, ain't nobody can take you."

"Get some sleep."

They turned in, weary and tired. The bed was creaky and worn, the mattress hard, but they slept well.

In the morning they had breakfast in the dining room, where they saw a lot of couples in their Sunday best. Ed Grange and his sister entered, moving to the long center table. That seemed to be his private spread. Jess decided to sit there next time.

They learned from the waiter that church was at ten, just thirty minutes away. Jess really enjoyed his eggs and steak. On the trail, eggs were a rare luxury, and even steak was uncommon.

"She's smilin' at you again," Sam remarked.

Jess tipped his hat to Elizabeth Grange. She was pretty and likeable, and a man could get interested in her if he had the time and the inclination. Jess fought that with everything he had.

As the Darringers stood up and started to leave, she turned to them. They paused near her chair.

"It's all over town this morning," she said.

"What's that, ma'am?" Sam asked innocently.

"About Jess Darringer and the Hatchers."

Grange seemed annoyed that she was talking to them. He merely acknowledged their presence, and his eyes were gleaming his dislike.

Jess and Sam tipped their hats and left the dining room. In the lobby, Sam grinned from ear to ear.

"All right," Jess said. "Spit it out."

"She's sure got a hankerin' for you."

Before they could head for the door, Lance Colby entered, followed by his wife, daughter, and Neal. The brothers paused and removed their hats.

Colby was grinning, his mustache curled back. Neal was arrogant, as usual. Lance's wife was as stuffy as before. Lorena was wearing a blue silk dress with white lace, and her hair was done up in curls. She was mighty pretty as she smiled at Jess and Sam.

Colby said, "I just heard about last night. That was one fine visit to the Hatchers."

"You got lucky, Darringer," Neal said. "That Red Hatcher is fast. He practices hours a day. You'll be seein' him again."

"Jess is a peaceful man," Sam told them. "If he's left alone, that is."

"He must've knowed what he was getting into," Neal said. "I don't think it was bein' brave. It was stupid."

"Something he learned from the Comanche," Sam continued. "I hope you never get around to callin' one of *them* stupid."

Neal glared at Sam, who was at ease and grinning.

"I'm glad you're coming to the ranch," Lorena said.

"Come along, Lorena," her mother cut in.

Lorena cast a smile at Jess as she followed her mother toward the dining room. Neal grunted something and went after them. Colby was still grinning, tickled plumb through.

"I'll see you boys in church," he said. "And tonight you can bed down in the bunkhouse. You just follow the wagon road west of town and head north."

They watched him saunter along behind his son. Then they turned and went outside onto the boardwalk. The morning sun was bright, but in the west, black clouds were moving in from the mountains.

"You know, we're gettin' mighty friendly with them folks," Sam said. "It won't be easy when we find the killers. And Lorena Colby won't like you much if you drag some of her brothers off."

"Nothin' I can do about that."

Pausing, they watched the marshal walking toward them, his grizzled mustache twitching. As he pushed his hat back, he looked all business.

"Good morning, Marshal," Jess said casually.

Clinton stopped in front of them. He hooked his thumbs in his gun belt and studied them a long moment before talking.

"Now listen to me, both of you. I've been workin' mighty hard to keep the Hatchers and Colbys apart. If they ever mix it up, this town will burn to the ground. Jess, I don't much appreciate your putting your fist in Red Hatcher's face."

"He was gonna shoot Jess," Sam told him.

"So I heard. But I also hear tell that you boys are goin' to work for Colby."

"We're also on our way to church," Jess said. "Are you comin'?"

Clinton hesitated, his mouth full of unspoken words. Finally he just shook his head and walked away, talking to himself. The brothers turned up the hill between the livery and the blacksmith shop. A greasy, swarthy man with a huge hammer hailed them as they passed his smithy.

"You the Darringers?"

Jess nodded.

"Feller over at the livery is waitin' to see you."

"He give a name?" Jess asked.

"Nope."

The brothers turned toward the livery, walking around front. The sun was in their eyes until they moved close to the barn. Jess checked his six-gun, then slid it back into the holster.

"You think it's an ambush?" Sam whispered.

"Just hang back."

Jess went into the livery first. It was empty of men except for the big, hairy-faced man seated on a rung of one of the ladders to the loft.

"Rocher," Jess said, surprised.

Sam entered, his gun hand relaxing now.

"Glad to see you fellas," the big man said.

"What are you doing here?"

"Well, Jess, it's like this. My eyes are gettin' mighty bad, but my hearin's pretty sharp. I got me a job here at the livery, and there's no tellin' what I might hear."

"What are you getting at?" Jess asked.

"Back on the trail, I heard you and your brother talkin' about what you got to do. I can help."

"But why?" Jess persisted.

"Because I owe you."

Jess swallowed. He was discovering that Rocher was indeed an honorable man. He didn't know what to say.

"It's a good idea," Sam ventured. "We appreciate it. In fact, why don't you come along to church?"

"Then everybody would know I was with you," Rocher said, taken aback.

It took a while, but they finally convinced Rocher it would do him good. Mumbling to himself, the big man walked some twenty feet behind them, out of the livery and up the hill. He pretended not to know them and fell behind, still leery of being hit with fire and brimstone.

Dark clouds were climbing over the Rockies in the west. Wagons and carriages were already lined up around the little church on the hillside. As they approached on foot, the Darringers saw Elizabeth Grange with her brother talking to some merchants and their wives. As soon as she saw them, she broke away and came over to greet them.

"It's a beautiful morning," she said, smiling. "But it may rain by nightfall."

"Winter will be early," Jess said.

"Something else you learned from the Comanche?" she asked, her smile more flirtatious than ever. "Yes, this is a very small town, Mr. Darringer."

Jess was flustered by her constant smile and twinkling eyes. He didn't know how to handle a conversation with her. He knew that Sam enjoyed his nervous reaction, and refused to look at him.

Grange came over to her side.

"You men hired on with Colby, I hear," he said. "He's a friend of mine. Anything you need, let me know."

"Will there ever be a railroad here?" Jess asked.

Grange looked annoyed. "As soon as enough is collected to get the spur up here. It's a town project."

"So these people will be payin' for their own spur?" Jess persisted.

"I tried to get General Palmer to invest in it," Grange said, more irritated. "He's too busy explorin' the way to some silver mines up north of here. May I ask if this is any of your business?"

"I'm a curious man."

Jess knew he was making an enemy, but Elizabeth didn't grasp the war between him and her brother. She was too busy flirting.

They all turned as the Colby wagon approached. Lorena was sitting between her father and mother. Neal was riding alongside.

"There's a whole lot more of them," Elizabeth said.

"But none so difficult as that old man," Grange added.

At that point Grange put on a cheerful face and went to greet the Colbys. He made a big display of helping Mrs. Colby and Lorena to climb down over the giant wheel. He then took Lorena's arm.

Pausing, Lorena smiled at Jess and Sam. She pulled free of Grange, who was further angered, so that she might walk over to the brothers. She was looking right at Jess, however.

"I told my father how you could sing and play so well, Mr. Darringer. Maybe you would favor us tomorrow night for supper and some music, you and your brother."

Jess swallowed hard, embarrassed. She was too much for him to handle. Too pretty, too much of a woman. She could ride and shoot like a man. He didn't know how to react to her. The only thing he knew for sure was that she smelled like sweet lilacs.

"We'd be mighty happy," Sam said, grinning.

Grange came to collect her, leaving Elizabeth standing there with a slight pout on her delicate lips. Then she recovered and, to Jess's surprise, took his arm. To save Jess, Sam took her other arm, and the three walked into the crowded church. They paused at the rear pew, where she left them to join the Colbys and her brother up front.

The preacher was a little man who indeed threw out a mouthful of fire and brimstone. Singing the hymns with the crowd, and with the music provided by an elderly lady on a tuneless organ, Jess kept his voice low. He wasn't used to town folks. His home was the land. Sam had a good voice, and he sang more freely.

It was the last hymn that surprised Jess. As Lorena stood up, her back to the crowd, the fiddle began to play sweet sounds, and her voice lifted in a glorious soprano that sent shivers up Jess's spine:

"Amazing Grace, how sweet the sound
That saved a wretch like me.
I once was lost, but now I'm found,
Was blind, but now I see."

The congregation stood and sang the other verses with her. It was beautiful. Jess looked across the aisle and saw Rocher sniffling back his tears.

Jess turned abruptly and went out the open door, fighting for air in the fading sunlight. The dark clouds were coming fast from the northwest. He took a deep breath of freedom.

Sam caught up with Jess as he walked away from the church.

"What got into you?" Sam asked.

"Nothing."

"Couldn't be that Lorena Colby's gettin' under your skin?"

Jess muttered some response, unable to look at Sam.

"Well, if she is, I wouldn't blame you," Sam continued as they moved down the hill. "I mean, just listenin' to her sing, that makes a man think of settin' a fire in the hearth and choppin' all the wood."

Jess walked faster, gritting his teeth. They reached the livery just as the first drops of rain fell. The sky was darkening. Black clouds were moving fast overhead.

"Gonna be a real storm," Jess predicted.

Before rounding the corner, they paused to look back at the little white church. Everyone was scrambling for wagons and horses.

Lorena and her mother were among the last to get out of the church and hurry to their wagon. Lance Colby about threw them up onto the wagon seat. He pulled a tarp around the women, released the foot brake, and set the team to moving and turning around.

Grange was busy bringing up a buggy near the church entrance where Elizabeth was waiting. People were in a mighty hurry. Rocher was running and jumping downhill.

As Jess and Sam started for the livery entrance, they learned why. Lightning flashed in the black sky. There was a rumble, and then heavy, giant drops of rain plunged earthward like an ocean turned upside down, flooding and beating everyone and everything. The brothers dived for the entrance.

"I'll be a cross-eyed mule!" Sam gasped as they stood just inside and watched the deluge.

"That creek only got about four feet to rise," Jess said.

"And it'll get right to the top," Potter said from behind. "But we only been flooded out once or twice."

"That's nice to know," Sam responded, grinning. "Jess, time to go."

"Maybe it'll slow down," Jess said.

"Not for hours," Potter predicted.

Rocher came charging inside. He was soaked through and cussing. He had fallen and rolled in the water, waited in the smithy, then run over. Potter just laughed. Jess and Sam tried to be sympathetic, but were grinning when they went to saddle up.

The bay was walking better now, and it would do all right in the wet dirt. The brothers pulled on their slickers and tugged their hats down low. They mounted and turned their reluctant horses to the outside weather.

The rain had slowed just enough to give them confidence. Riding up the street, they saw only the backs of people racing for cover. Only horses and mules stood in the rain, tied to the railings, heads down.

They reached the wagon road just past the lone saloon at the west end of the street. The tracks left by the Colby wagon were filling with water. Crossing the first rise, they faced a series of rolling hills ahead of them. They saw no other riders or wagons. The pines and aspen were away from the trail, so they didn't worry too much as lightning flashed in the black sky.

But the rain became heavy again, pounding them and running off their mounts like gallons of water spilled on every inch.

"Just like home," Sam complained.

As they rode over the next hill, they saw the Colby wagon tipped sideways, the right rear wheel broken and in the mud. The women were standing aside, the tarp over them. The old man and Neal were trying to right the wagon. Jess and Sam rode up to them and dismounted.

"If you got an ax in the wagon," Jess said, "we'll cut a pole and make a crutch, like a travois."

Within half an hour they were raising the back axle and placing rocks under it. Jess and Sam attached the pole under the rear hub and over the front wheel axle, using ropes to make the right rear of the wagon into a partial, though uncertain, travois.

Sooner than expected, the women were back

on the wagon seat with Colby, suitably impressed. Neal rode ahead, annoyed as usual. The Darringers brought up the rear.

The team felt the drag of the bouncing pole, but they gallantly pulled onward, their minds set on the barn.

Before dark, they sighted the ranch buildings. A stable and sheds were off to the right, next to a series of corrals. Beyond were the tack room and a long, rambling bunkhouse. High on another hill, to the left, was the ranch house, a great frame building with a porch and full veranda. Tall, shimmering aspen and several pine trees provided shade, but now they could draw lightning. To each side of the ranch house there were two other buildings that looked like houses, but they were difficult to see in the downpour.

The team fought its way up to the main house with the Colbys, while the Darringers headed for the barn. They found empty stalls for their mounts. After unsaddling and rubbing them down with some old sacks, they fed the animals and took their gear, pausing in the doorway. Oceans of water were swirling past them.

"Run for it!" Jess said.

Through the downpour and ankle-high water they scrambled for the bunkhouse, dashing inside and then kicking the door closed. Having caught their breath, they paused to look around. It was a long building with enough bunks for forty men. Gear and bridles were spread about or hanging from wall hooks. Rain sounded like stampeding cattle on the roof.

Five of the men were present, four of them playing cards at one of the two tables, and they gave the brothers a nod of their heads. They were as close to the stove as they could get. The fifth, a hefty man with a fat grin, came forward.

"You the new hands? There's two empty bunks way down the end on your right. Afeared it's a long way from the heat."

"I'm Jess and that's Sam."

"They call me Kansas," the man said, shaking their hands and rattling off the names of the other men.

The brothers carried their gear down to the empty bunks. They were glad to take off their slickers and catch their breath.

"Supper's at sundown," Kansas said as he joined them. "We got us one fine cook. Old Curly used to be on the cattle trail."

"Curly Spicks? Little guy with no hair?" Jess asked.

"That's him."

Jess grinned. "Now I really am hungry."

"And sleepy," Sam said, flopping on the lower bunk.

Rather than fight over the bunk, Jess made

his way up the ladder and spread out. Kansas left them to fall asleep in their weariness.

It wasn't easy for Jess, however. His thoughts kept churning over why he was here. He had to find the killers, even if they were Colbys, but all the while, he kept hearing Lorena's sweet voice. He had never met anyone like her. Just the same, when his job was done, he was lighting out of here as fast as he could ride. This he kept telling himself, even as sleep came.

Chapter Five

AT suppertime Sunday night, Jess and Sam dragged themselves out of bed. A lot of hands had come and gone while they slept. Kansas was still there, pulling on his woolen coat.

One other man was in view, a tall, husky gent with a handlebar mustache and pale eyes. His hat was shoved back from a wide forehead. Kansas introduced him as Gibbs, the foreman.

"I was talkin' to Mr. Colby," Gibbs said to the brothers. "He tells me you'll be working under him, seein's how your job is to catch them rustlers. They want you to supper tomorrow night. I got you until then. Some green broncs. That bother you any?"

"Nope," Sam said with an easy grin.

"I also hear from Miss Colby that you can play that there squeezebox and sing a little," Gibbs said to Jess. "This bein' Sunday night, I'd take it as a favor if you'd play a few songs for the men."

Jess nodded. This was his kind of place, and

these men were just like the hands on the trail. He liked being around them.

The brothers followed Kansas and Gibbs into the now-quieter rain and circled the bunkhouse to the cook shed, which was only a few feet away. Inside, two long tables were lined with nearly thirty men, all loud and full of spirit. Jess felt at home, and he and Curly had a few words about old times. Then he asked Kansas about the other Colbys while they ate.

"You met Neal, I take it," the hefty man said. "Up on either side of the main house, there are a group of other houses built for the sons and their wives. The other brothers, all six of 'em, are just like Neal."

"How's that?" Jess persisted.

His voice lowered, Kansas continued: "Ornery, quick to fight, pigheaded. Two of 'em, I wouldn't turn my back on. I figure they been up to some dirty work. Not here, where the old man can see, of course."

"Which are they?"

"Hack and Harley." Kansas ended his story as Gibbs gave him a stern look.

When the men were all settled down in the bunkhouse, a young man named Hooper brought out his guitar. Jess sat near him with his squeezebox.

"Sure hope you can sing better than Hooper," one cowhand said as the others laughed.

Hooper grinned, his round face full of humor. Jess let him play a fast jig on his own. Then they joined their music in an old trail song. There were many verses, and as Jess sang, the men listened quietly, dreaming and enjoying their memories of roundups.

The night grew long. More songs were sung. On some, the men joined in. Sometimes Jess played the guitar, at which he was adept, while Hooper played with the concertina. It was a pleasurable evening. Between tunes, Jess told them stories of the cattle trails on the Chisholm and the Western.

They all slept well that night, but in the morning, they hit the saddle before dawn, when it was still raining softly. Most of the men were out riding herd, looking for strays and stock in trouble.

Jess and Sam both stayed with Gibbs and Kansas, taking turns on the hurricane decks of the wild broncs that Colby had just bought. One such bellowing beast leaped the fence and took Jess bounding up the hillside, bucking and fighting all the way.

At the top, north of the big ranch house, the animal came to a halt, panting and shaking its head. In both directions, Jess saw the other houses. He had yet to meet Neal's brothers.

The bronc charged forward and down the other side of the hill. There they were met by a fence and small stable. The bronc reared and spun, but was so worn out that it couldn't move farther.

Curious, Jess looked over the three empty corrals. In one corral's opening to the middle of the three stalls, he saw a black gelding. In the first corral's stall, there was a magnificent chestnut stallion with a white mane and its ears pulled back. It tossed its head in defiance.

Taken by the animal, Jess urged the bronc up to the fence. Immediately, the stallion charged, skidding up to the fence and biting the air. It was well bred and chunky all over, but with lean, fast legs. Its head had a gentle dip above the nostrils. The eyes were fiery black. Tossing and kicking, it spun about and headed back to the barn, wild, untamed, beautiful.

As he turned the bronc back over the hill, Jess grinned to himself. That stallion was the horse he wanted.

Back at the corral, pulling his hat down tight, he reined the bronc inside the fence line, where Gibbs was grinning from ear to ear.

"You sure can sit a horse, Jess."

"Thanks."

"And your brother too."

But at that moment, Sam hit the mud and slid to a halt as his bronc took off in a series of spinning bucks. He looked embarrassed.

"Let's call it a day," Gibbs said. "You're all wet and tired, and you boys are set for supper at the main house. Better get cleaned up. And don't forget your squeezebox."

"What about that chestnut stallion?" Jess asked.

"You saw him, did you?" Gibbs grunted. "Well, he ain't good for nothin' but breedin' the mares. No one can ride him."

Jess felt a challenge and a wish to own the animal.

As he and Sam shaved and cleaned up for supper, the other men were coming in, tired and wet. It was noisy in the bunkhouse as the brothers left. Under his slicker Jess reluctantly carried his squeezebox in its leather case.

"Did you notice?" Jess said, hunching in the drizzle. "Not one of them cared that our name is Darringer."

"I noticed. Some good boys in there."

They walked deep in mud and swirling water. Upon the porch, they found sacks to clean off their boots. When they were ready, Jess knocked.

A small Indian woman wearing a dark blue dress opened the door. A Comanche, she wore her hair in braids drawn back from her square face. She was probably in her fifties, and she was able to speak English well.

"Enter, please," she said, her black eyes flashing.

She pointed them through a hallway, which was full of coats and hats, to a distant parlor.

Jess and Sam watched her disappear as they hung up their hats and slickers. Jess set his squeezebox on a table.

"Comanche," Sam said. "You figure she knows we're Texans?"

"You worried?"

Sam gave a nervous laugh as Jess led the way down the hallway to the parlor. It was another world, with a sea of men, women, and children, but no Lorena.

Lush crimson drapes hung on the great windows. The carpet was the same color and inches deep. A fire burned in the great stone hearth. The furniture was stuffed and soft, crimson and white. There was a lot of shining walnut wood. In the corner was a tall, narrow piano.

Jess looked at the men and could recognize at once Neal's six brothers. They had the same large nose—their father's, most likely—and the same light brown hair, gleaming brown eyes, and suspicious looks.

Two of the brothers caught his attention. They were not surrounded by their wives and children, and were inspecting a new carbine. Both had grim, narrow mouths.

Lance Colby came out and introduced them around. The only names that stuck were Hack and Harley, the two mean ones. Neal was there, but his gruffness was mostly for show.

It was obvious that the other two took pleasure in theirs.

Jess had never misread a trail, a bronc, or a man. He could see that Neal was in love with Lorena, probably the reason he was unmarried. She had never been adopted, and so was free to marry Neal, but she regarded him as a brother.

There was a lot of talk about Texas, but no one there mentioned having been there last July. Everything was spoken in small talk. The wives, mostly demure and prim, had nothing to say. The children, noisy at times, were ignored.

Dinner was a blessing. Even though the silent Comanche was serving the table, the brothers enjoyed the good meat, potatoes, and delicious biscuits. They were seated at the foot of the table among wives and children. The Colby men and Lorena were up near the father, who sat at the head. Lorena's foster mother sat on his left, opposite Lorena.

"So we're gonna have our own spur," Lance Colby was saying. "I figure on renaming the north side of the town to Colbyville. Right now, my sons don't like newcomers, but they ain't thinkin' straight. I see us as havin' the biggest city this side of the Rockies. Why, folks from Denver will come here just to see our opera house, as soon as it's built."

"We'll all prosper," his wife added.

"Come spring, the surveyors will be here," Colby said.

"Why not now?" Jess asked.

"I figure they must be busy. Grange told me it'd be spring. But we don't care, as long as we get our railroad."

"You trust him?" Jess asked.

"Since he'd give most anything to wed my daughter and get his foot on this spread and his fingers in our holdings, I reckon I do."

"What's it to you?" Hack growled at Jess.

"Hack," his mother scolded, "Mr. Darringer's a guest."

The conversation switched to Denver, with Neal praising it as a booming city, set with fancy new inventions.

"But they banned *Tom Sawyer,*" Jess complained.

"Who's that?" Neal growled.

Jess grinned, and to his surprise, Lorena's foster mother was delighted with Jess's remark.

Jess soon learned that he and Lorena's mother had a pleasure in common—books. They were soon discussing, across the length of the table, Mark Twain's *Tom Sawyer,* which had been banned a year ago in Denver. Both had read *The Circuit Rider* by Eggleston, about a pioneer preacher. Jess ignored the glares of the Colby brothers and enjoyed the woman's knowledge and wit. He caught Lorena and Lance Colby staring at him, more than once.

Dinner was over all too soon. Jess took one last slice of pound cake and gulp of strong coffee. The men went into the parlor as the women assisted in cleaning up. Hack and Harley rolled a smoke. Some had whiskey, which Jess and Sam declined.

"You too good to drink with us?" Harley demanded.

Colby stepped in quickly. "Son, it wouldn't hurt you to have a bit of moderation."

There was talk of the ranch, which apparently was large enough to support nearly nine thousand head in the hills alone, with another herd on the mesa. They were concerned about early winter and snow. They all knew that cattle breathing snow could die from suffocation.

There was also talk of rustling. Five more head had disappeared. Hack and Harley had brazenly ridden to the Hatcher range, but had been turned back by forty riders, or so they claimed.

"Clinton can't do much," Colby growled. "He's just one man and we gotta have proof. That's where Jess and Sam come in."

"Well, we got a lot more'n a few thousand acres," Harley said. "How they gonna cover that?"

"I told you," the old man said. "Jess is a tracker."

There was a lot of skepticism among the brothers, mostly Hack, Harley, and Neal. The others were more domesticated, coming to life as their children charged in to attack them.

The Comanche brought a tray with cups of hot coffee, which the Darringers readily accepted. The silent woman looked at Sam and Jess a long time before serving the others.

"Got her when we first came," Colby said. "She was sick and lost in the snow, abandoned."

"She knows we're Texans," Sam said.

"So what's so great about Texas, anyhow?" Hack demanded. "All you got down there is them longhorns. We've had to breed 'em into purebreds to get any meat on 'em."

"You can say anything you want about the longhorns," Jess said, "but you leave Texas out of it."

"Don't get sore," Colby said. "They was just joshin' you. By the way, you ain't forgot my offer to pick out any horse on the place, and it's yours to own."

"What's this?" Hack growled.

"I ain't givin' your own horses away," the old man said. "But Jess can pick out any ranch horse he takes a fancy to. We owe him that, for savin' Lorena."

"Why not pick one out for him?" Neal grunted.

"Well, Jess?" the old man persisted.

"Ordinarily," Jess said, "I'd look at one of the cow ponies, but I saw one I'd sure like to put a rope on. When we were ridin' broncs, I saw a chestnut stallion."

Colby's face was strained. "We mostly use him at stud. No one has ever been able to ride him."

"*I* can," Jess told him.

"That horse cost me plenty," Colby said, thoughtful, "and he's well bred, that's a fact. But if you agree to keep on breedin' the mares while you're workin' here, he's yours. Only one condition. You got to ride him to a standstill, without spurs."

The Colby sons laughed heartily. Their father was grinning as he added, "My boys all tried to ride him."

"It's a deal," Jess agreed. He leaned back with his coffee, startled by Lorena standing at his side. She had heard the bargain, and she looked down at him with the same delicious smile that curled up his hair at the back of his neck.

"You want Comanche?" she asked.

"That his name?"

"Men have been crippled trying to ride him."

"I'll take that chance."

"Brave man," Neal said, snickering. "We'll be scraping you out of the mud with a shovel."

"I want to work with him first," Jess said.

"The Comanche way," the Indian woman said as she brought another pot of coffee. She paused, looking directly at Jess. Her gaze went right through him and seared his spine. Then she turned and disappeared again.

Lorena could see Jess's discomfort. She smiled as she went to sit on the couch by her father. The other women came in and told their husbands that the children had to go to bed.

"I wanted to hear this gunfighter play his little toy box," Hack said. His timid wife stood near him, waiting. Finally he stood up.

"Well," Harley said, "we won't miss much. He probably sounds like a cow bellowin'."

Jess watched the way Hack and Harley were unpleasant to their women. Brutal and harsh, they were the type who could walk over a woman and not look back. The hair tightened on the back of his neck. If these were the men who had murdered Sue Ellen, he wasn't sure he could just wait for the marshal.

In a matter of time, all had left the house but Neal, the only unmarried son, Lorena and her mother, and Lance Colby. That was easier for Jess to handle than the whole clan. As it was, he was plenty nervous and hoping they would let him forget the whole thing. Instead, they were gathering around to listen.

"What about the piano?" he asked.

"Lorena plays," her mother said, "but she's

still very tired. Tonight we want to hear your Texas songs."

"I'd rather *she* was singing," Jess said, uncomfortable.

Good old Sam went out and retrieved the squeezebox. Jess loved to play and sing around the campfire, but not in a fancy house full of strangers. But he liked Lance and his daughter, and he saw smiles from Mrs. Colby. He also wanted to keep them off guard while his manhunt continued. The squeezebox would certainly keep him from looking like a gunfighter.

Seated in the big stuffed chair, box in hand, Jess swallowed hard. Lorena and her parents settled on the couch. Sam sat cross-legged in another chair. Neal sat farther away, arms stiffly folded. The fire was burning bright and spitting, crackling its own tune.

"Come on, son," Colby said. "If I can give up Comanche, you can sing us a song."

"Yeah, sing for your supper," Neal grunted.

Jess felt his mouth going dry. Whenever he was around Lorena, the song that came to mind was always "Red River Valley." He began to squeeze out the soft ballad. It was hard for him to sing with these strangers. Playing the music, he found he had no voice. He could only stare into the crackling fire. But Lorena was suddenly singing, sweet and clear:

"There never could be such a longing,
In the heart of a poor cowboy's breast,
As dwells in the heart you are breaking,
As I wait in my home in the West."

Jess sang the chorus, but he played the next two verses without singing. Embarrassed, he wondered what he was doing here. He concentrated on the fire in the hearth, trying to forget that the Colbys were watching him. At last, he found his voice:

"They will bury me where we have
     wandered,
In the hills where the daffodils grow,
When you're gone from the Red River
     Valley,
For I can't live without you, I know."

Jess played but didn't sing another chorus. The words were getting to him, reminding him of why he was here. Lorena and her parents clapped as the song ended. Bored, Neal excused himself and left the parlor.

Jess couldn't keep his hands from shaking. Lorena's voice had the power of sending disastrous shivers up his spine. He couldn't look at her as he played and sang several trail tunes, mostly about stampedes and Indians. Closing the box, he swallowed hard and said, "Reckon I got no more in me tonight."

"It was a pleasure," Lorena said.

"Thank you, Jess," her mother added.

The two women left the room, but Lorena glanced back, catching Jess's eye. Her smile was as sweet as apple cider. Alone with Lance Colby and Sam, Jess shoved the box back into its leather case.

"No need to hurry off," Colby said. "Tomorrow you take your time. Fool around with the stallion if you want. This rain ain't gonna let you do much trackin'."

"Sometimes it's easier in the rain," Jess told him.

"If Jess rides this chestnut, it's his?" Sam asked.

"Bill of sale and all," Colby promised. "What you did for my daughter, Jess, I can never repay. If you hadn't come along, the posse would never have known to leave the main trail. I pretty much figure you saved her life."

Jess was uncomfortable with praise. He and Sam stood up, and got ready to leave.

"I ain't blind, you know," Colby added. "I see how my daughter's taken with you, but I don't want you gettin' any ideas."

"I ride alone," Jess assured him.

"We've kind of sheltered her on the ranch. We sent her to finishing school. She's barely twenty-one. Some fellers have come all the way from Denver to call on her, and there are some who got their eye on the mine and this ranch. But you fellas are gunfighters, and her ma has her heart set on a gentleman. No offense."

"None taken," Jess said, taking up his squeezebox. "All I want is that chestnut stallion."

Lance Colby seemed relieved, and he rose to walk to the door with them.

On the porch, in their hats and slickers, with the door closed behind them, Sam started to laugh.

"What's so blasted funny?" Jess glared out at the heavy rain.

"Well, he's worried about you and Lorena when you got no use for women."

Jess grunted as they stepped down into the rain, mud, and wet grass. Water whirled around their boots as they hurried downhill.

"I'll tell you one thing," Sam said. "The Colby brothers got no use for us." Then, before they entered the bunkhouse, he added, "It's also plenty obvious that either Lorena ain't told them about our reasons for bein' here, or she did and they're all innocent."

"They may just be sneaky about it," Jess said.

"If you're right, we'd better be watchin' over our shoulders."

They scrambled in out of the rain. Most of

the men were asleep. Kansas was snoring, his hat rising up and down on his belly. Jess and Sam warmed themselves at the stove before making their way through a pile of gear to get to their bunks.

Sam fell asleep first. Jess was still thinking about what Sam had said. He couldn't understand why Lorena might not have told her family. On the other hand, if she had told them and none was guilty, that would make it mighty hard to find the killers. In fact, it could be that the guilty raiders had no intention of returning to Buzzard's Creek. Worse, they might never have been here. Maybe it was time to trust the marshal.

Jess slept restlessly, and awoke often. The rain was heavy on the roof, but in the morning it was quiet. The men stirred before dawn and headed for the cook shed, Jess and Sam following. Breakfast was good and hot, the men were in good spirits, and the cook gave extra helpings to everyone.

After the other men rode out, Jess and Sam walked over the hill, slipping around in the mud, to take a look at the chestnut stallion. The sun was warm, but the wind was icy. It was a cloudless day that made a man glad to be alive.

At the corral, the stallion charged out to take a look at them. As it spun and snorted, Jess and Sam leaned on the fence and grinned at it. But Jess's grin faded as he thought of his black swimming horse and the way it had fought him all the time. Maybe that was why he liked the stallion. It was full of fire and willfulness. Abruptly, the animal came up to them and tossed its head.

Sam said, "I think he likes attention."

"He'll get plenty of it," Jess assured him.

In the days that followed, Jess worked with the horse whenever he and Sam were not out scouting. The stallion was broken to lead already, and was amenable to being groomed.

Jess had a way with animals, and he had learned all of the stallion's pleasure spots. Comanche had started to nuzzle him more and more, eating from his hand, watching for him and running out to meet him.

He hated to leave Comanche to go scouting, but he and Sam spent long hours in the cold wind that week. There were no signs of intruders.

On Friday afternoon Jess and Sam reined up on one of the thousand hills. Leaning on the pommel of his saddle, Jess stroked the neck of the ranch sorrel he was riding.

As he straightened, a bullet whistled past his face, almost searing his mouth. Jerking back and spinning his horse, six-gun in hand, he scanned the surrounding terrain.

"Up there," Sam said, pointing with his rifle.

They set their heels to their horses and headed straight for the ridge at the foot of the mesa.

Chapter Six

RACING their ponies, heads down, Jess and Sam darted through the trees and rocks, heading for the ridge that was the forefront to the mesa country. They crossed a narrow, fast-running creek, and skidding their mounts into heavy cover in the woods, they swung from the saddle, leaving the horses ground-tied as they moved through the trees and brush. A woodpecker scolded them and flew away.

Jess could still taste the whistle of the bullet that had nearly singed his lips. Grimacing, he led the climb up through the rocks. He was breathing hard when he neared the top, figuring that the shooter was long gone.

At last, he was climbing onto the barren top of the rocky ridge. There was no one there. Sam joined him from some twenty feet away and they looked in all directions. No sign of a rider.

"Could it have come from the mesa?" Sam asked.

97

"Not likely, unless someone's got an old Sharps."

"Or wears moccasins."

"Maybe it didn't come from up here at all."

They retreated from the ridge and searched the woods. Away from where they had ridden, they found prints of a horse's hooves, along with an empty cartridge.

"Probably a Winchester," Jess said as he knelt. "Fresh prints. Shod with a narrow shoe on the right front hoof. See how the wall has overhung and split?"

They followed the tracks, but lost them on a cattle trail where everything was hoof-sized mudholes. They rode south until they connected with Kansas and Hooper.

"Didn't see anyone," Kansas said. "But the way these hills go up and down, that ain't surprising."

"Let us know when you're gonna ride Comanche," Hooper said with a grin.

As the Darringers rode on south, Jess was thinking how every man on the place was licking his chops at the thought of someone being bucked off Comanche once more.

So it was on Saturday morning that about thirty men lined the corrals at the stables back of the main house. Among them were Lance Colby and his sons. From a respectful distance, Lorena stood on the hillside with her Indian maid.

The men were literally smacking their lips, and Jess could see expectation in Neal Colby's eyes. The man wanted to see him dumped in front of Lorena. And Hack and Harley just didn't like him at all.

Although Comanche had been saddled many times before, the animal reached back to bite at the blanket and gear. Jess kept free of the gnashing teeth.

"Listen," he said quietly to the animal. "There's a heap of folks wantin' to see me bucked off. So if we're friends, maybe you won't be pleasin' 'em."

Comanche stood quietly as Jess stroked the powerful neck and shoulders. He'd been told that the stallion wouldn't do anything until he was sitting in the saddle, and then a hurricane would be unleashed. With his hand on the bridle and reins, he slowly put his foot in the stirrup and lifted himself onto the saddle. Comanche shuddered. The big Mexican horn was always tempting, but Jess just sat down, waiting. When nothing happened, Jess set his heels to the stallion, gently. The animal moved forward and began to walk around the corral. Holding his breath, Jess leaned forward to stroke the big neck.

Any minute now, the horse could hit the sky. He could feel the power in the animal. It became a part of him as he rode. Still, nothing happened.

There was great disappointment among the spectators, and they began to drift away. Neal had scowled before turning from the corral. Lance Colby was grinning. The other brothers were not impressed.

But up on the hill, the Comanche woman was silently approving Jess's way of gaining the animal's confidence. And Lorena, her yellow hair shining in the sunlight, stood watching with her arms folded and her skirts whirling in the wind.

Jess felt proud. But as the animal shuddered, Jess tensed. Again the animal shook all over and tossed his head. But there was no buck in him. He and Jess had become as one. They had talked with each other. They had held a conversation.

Sam opened the gate, and Jess rode the stallion out of the corral and up onto the hill, reining up near Lorena.

"He's so beautiful," she said, smiling.

"Tell your father to write up that bill of sale."

"I will."

Jess rode over the hill and down toward the other corrals. Just his luck, there would be a mare in heat, setting off the stallion. But nothing happened. Even Jess was a little disappointed, and he rode back over the hill. Lorena and the maid were gone. Only Sam and Lance Colby remained at the corral.

Jess dismounted inside the fence, and then stroked the animal's head and neck. He unsaddled and removed the bridle, letting the animal prance around free. The horse kept returning to nuzzle Jess.

"Never seen anything like it," Colby said, impressed.

"Tomorrow too soon to collect?" Jess asked.

"No," the rancher said with a grin.

"Sam tell you about the split hoof mark?"

"Sure did. He also said there were no such prints in our corrals. Could be a Hatcher."

"That's just what I'm going to find out," Jess said.

That afternoon Jess and Sam rode into town. Jess didn't ride Comanche away from the ranch yet. He wanted to spend more time with the stallion before he did much riding. Instead, he rode a black gelding.

Jess and Sam checked the street on the north side of the creek, looking for prints of the split hoof, without success. They asked the smithy, but he hadn't reshod such a horse that day. The livery corrals revealed no such sign.

Frustrated, the brothers went to the big hotel for an early supper. They arrived before the Granges and seated themselves at the long center table. The waiter just shook his head. Other diners were curious.

The brothers were already eating their steak

when Grange and his sister arrived. Annoyed, the railroad man sat far down the long table and glared at them for intruding on his private realm.

Elizabeth, however, wearing blue silk and a ribbon in her dark hair, came over to Jess. The brothers rose to their feet and tipped their hats.

"I'm curious," she said, smiling. "Why do cowboys keep their hats on all the time?"

They removed their hats, embarrassed.

"They can't even walk very far down the street," she said. "They get on their horses instead. You're a very strange lot."

"Elizabeth," her brother called.

She signaled him to wait, then moved closer to Jess, her fingers soft on his coat sleeve. Her voice was sweet and persuasive.

"I thought you'd be calling on me, Jess Darringer."

He swallowed as she squeezed his arm before leaving. The brothers pulled their hats on and sat down. Exhausted from her nearness, Jess was sure ready for the open range.

Finished eating, the brothers lingered over their coffee and talked quietly about Texas. As Grange left the table abruptly, Elizabeth came to sit at Jess's side.

"You must think me terribly forward," she said, smiling, "but, you see, I have this problem. Ever since I was a little girl, I've been unafraid. I just break all convention."

"You're to be admired for that," Jess said.

"Also, I do it to make Ed furious."

"Keep at it," Jess advised, grinning.

"You don't like my brother, do you?"

"No, ma'am."

"Tell me, Mr. Darringer, why did you and your brother come to Buzzard's Creek?"

Jess decided it was time to spread the word a little more. The sooner the killers heard, the faster this search would end.

"There was this girl in Texas," he said. "She was teaching school and living alone. Four or five men came by in the night and murdered her. One of them had a paper that had the name of this town."

"Did you know her well?" she asked, her dark eyes glistening. There was a growing sadness in her pretty face.

Jess nodded. He was seeing a new side to Elizabeth, and he liked her better now.

"And that's why you're here?" she asked.

Again Jess nodded. Just then, her brother returned, and she rejoined him at the far end of the table.

After dinner, the brothers went out into the moonlight. Lamplight from windows and above doorways added to the glow.

"Do you think Grange is plannin' to take off with the town's money?" Sam asked.

"I figure he's got to weigh the amount of the

money and losin' his job against a chance to marry Lorena."

"I'm bettin' he's got no chance o' that."

"There's a light in the jail. Let's stop."

"You trust Clinton?"

"Got to keep spreadin' the word, or we won't learn anything around here," Jess said.

"We're sure askin' for a shot in the back."

The brothers paused outside the marshal's office. Rocher, his hairy face set in a grin, was approaching them. Settled on his chubby nose was a pair of spectacles.

"Look at me," Rocher said. "I can see. It sure does a feller good to go to church."

"We're headed for the wild side as soon as we see the marshal," Jess said. "You're welcome to come along."

Rocher agreed readily, because he was tired of being by himself. The three of them entered the marshal's office. He was dozing behind his desk in a corner. The wall was plastered with crude posters of wanted men. He had a small iron stove between his desk and the bunk, set along the left wall. In the back to the right, the two cells were empty.

As Jess slammed the door behind them, Clinton jumped up, hand on his holster, and blinked himself awake. "That's no way to come in here," he growled.

The brothers just grinned and sat at his desk. Rocher stayed near the door. Within minutes they had filled him in on the July murder of Sue Ellen, including the details of the locket and music box. They told him about the shooting on Friday and the split hoof, and handed over the empty cartridge.

Clinton opened his drawer and brought out a fistful of new reward posters. He flicked through them until he found the one he had remembered. He read it aloud: " 'Wanted dead or alive. The men who murdered Sue Ellen Cambridge on the night of July 16, 1877, near the town of Austin, Texas. Fifteen-hundred dollar reward.' "

Jess winced. Was that all a young woman was worth?

He reached inside his jacket for his mother's letter and brought it out to retrieve the receipt. He showed it to the marshal, told him where it was found, and asked him to keep it locked up as potential evidence.

"Don't prove much," Clinton said. "It could have been stolen." He studied them. "So you come to town lookin' for that chipped hoof."

"The evidence is out there, hard and fast," Jess said. "Been lookin' in town, but no sign of it. We're on our way to the south side."

"You won't see much of prints in the dark."

"Jess will," Sam assured him.

"Seems to me," Clinton said, "any man who goes into Hatcher country lookin' for a fight is goin' to get it."

"You coming?" Jess asked.

"Now, if I was to go amblin' over there with you, they'd figure we was in cahoots. Might be better if no one knows we been talkin' about this. But if I hear shootin', I'll come runnin'."

The brothers left the marshal's office wondering if he was on their side or the Colbys'. Now they had fed further information about their purpose here to a man who might well run to the Colbys.

The brothers caught up their horses, but Rocher was on foot, following along as they crossed the bridge. Turning to their right, they rode to the saloon where the Hatchers hung out.

The three men paused outside the noisy saloon. The round piano player was still pounding the keys in a lively tune. Smoke and noise came through the swinging doors. Lanterns were hung outside the entrance.

Jess walked into the street and kneeled. Even in the poor light he could see the split hoof mark. Finally he found the horse, a bay gelding with white stockings. A hand-tooled saddle was on its back with the initials R.H., maybe for Red Hatcher.

The brothers and their companion entered the saloon. At the first table on their right, the Hatchers were having their card game. Bull Hatcher, husky of build, looked up as they passed. His beard twitched as he glared at them. Seated across from his father, Red studied his cards and didn't look up.

The saloon was filled with Hatcher cowhands, all having a drink or playing poker. At the bar, Jess, Sam, and Rocher stood a few feet apart, leaning on the hard walnut and keeping their eyes on the mirror. Jess had forgotten what a big man Rocher was, towering between the brothers with his broad shoulders.

Jess and Sam ordered cider. Rocher had a beer.

Red Hatcher was suddenly standing up and throwing his cards down. "Somebody's cheatin'!"

His father growled, "You're talkin' about your own brothers."

Red kicked his chair aside and turned toward the bar. As he saw the Darringers, his red face and beady eyes came to life, and his wide mouth twisted in a sneer.

Slowly, Jess turned to look at him. Rocher and Sam also turned around. The music stopped. The room went silent.

Knowing he had the stage, Red swaggered forward, his right hand resting on the butt of his holstered Colt. He stopped six feet away, having learned his lesson.

"What're you Colby men doing here?" he demanded.

"What were you doing on Colby land yesterday?" Jess countered. "That horse of yours oughta be at the smithy, getting reshod. Or maybe you're the fool who put a narrow shoe on that hoof so it'd overhang and crack."

Red's face turned redder. There was a definite hush in the saloon.

"Did you come over there just to take a shot at us?" Jess asked. "Or were you using a runnin' iron?"

Red's fingers were closing and opening.

"Back off, son," Bull said. "I already done told you, we're pickin' our own time to take care o' them Darringers."

"I don't like waitin'," Red said, grimacing.

Everyone behind them suddenly left his seat and scrambled to the sides to be out of the line of fire. Even the Hatchers slid their chairs back toward the wall.

"Those four men you helped kill," Red snarled at Jess. "They were my cousins. We owe you, Darringer."

"The only thing I want from you," Jess said calmly, "is a walk to the jail. For attempted murder."

"No one's gonna believe you," Red told him.

"That mud's pretty dry by now," Jess said. "There'll be a mighty fine picture of your horse's hoof. I figure that would convince the jury."

"I got my own convincin', right here." Red patted his holster. "You wanta try me?"

"I just want you in jail," Jess told him.

"Nobody's takin' my son anywhere!" Bull roared, rising. "I'm gettin' mighty tired of you Darringers. Now get out of here."

Jess moved away from Rocher, keeping his right hand near his holster. Taking their cue from Bull, the fifteen or so Hatcher cowhands moved forward slowly. There was still no one between Red and the swinging doors. Realizing that a fight could destroy his play, Red stiffened. His beady eyes flashed. He drew swiftly.

But Jess's six-gun had leaped into his hand. His shot struck Red's gunhand. Blood splattered. The gun went flying. Red yelped.

It was then that the Hatchers and their men charged the Darringers and Rocher. In the noisy and bloody fight, Rocher proved to be the bull elephant, picking men up as if they were puppies and throwing them in all directions. Jess slammed his fist into every face that came his way. Lighter but quicker, Sam was enjoying the fight, dodging and hitting hard, and getting hit back.

A bottle slammed past Jess's face as he tried to get to Red. He heard Bull's roar. Rocher and the big man came together, struggling, hitting, and cussing. Rocher lifted Bull and threw him across the room.

As the brawl raged on, there were soon only seven men still fighting—the Darringers, Rocher, and Bull and two of his wiry sons. The other men lay on the floor or were trying to get up. Red was headed for the door.

Just then Clinton appeared, and Red backed away.

Firing a barrel of his shotgun into the air, Clinton glared around the room as the fighting stopped. Rocher gave Bull one last shove that sent him reeling against a table.

"What's goin' on here?" the marshal demanded.

"I found that split hoof," Jess said. "It belongs to Red Hatcher, who just drew on me."

"He's lyin'!" Bull yelled, furious.

"I figure," Jess said, "that attempted murder oughta put your boy away for at least five years. Sound about right, Marshal?"

Clinton weighed the situation. He had one more shell in his shotgun and his six-gun was in its holster. There was a room full of Hatchers, and his only allies were Jess, Rocher, and Sam.

Bull was another foot high as he hunched up in his anger. "Marshal, you get out o' here!"

"Sorry, Mr. Hatcher," Clinton said. "There's evidence of Red's horse out there where the shot was fired."

"Don't mean nothing," Bull said. "Prints could've been made anytime."

"On Colby land?" Jess asked.

"He's got a point," Clinton said. "He

could've been there, but someone else could've fired the shot."

Jess was furious, but he knew Clinton was right. There wasn't enough evidence to convince a jury that Red Hatcher was the one who had tried to kill him. Evidence placed him in the area. That was all.

Bull drew himself up to his full height. "Now, Marshal, if you're finished, we'll get back to our cards."

"I need a doctor," Red said, a bandanna wrapped around his bleeding right hand. His face was redder than ever; his beady eyes were hot.

"Mighty fast draw," Rocher said to Jess.

"You fellas move on out," Clinton told them.

"I got something else to say," Jess said, his voice rising. "Four or five men from this town rode through Texas last July. They killed a woman. My brother and I plan to find those men and see 'em hanged."

His words hung in the stillness. He looked around at the sea of hostile faces. Red's pink face was twisted in a scowl. Bull's eyes narrowed, his hate for Jess obvious.

"Move on out," Clinton said once more.

Reluctantly, the Darringers and Rocher walked past the still-fallen cowhands into the fresh night air. The lawman backed to the swinging doors, then outside.

The four men strode down the sidewalk to the Darringer horses.

"Sorry," Clinton apologized, "but he was right. You didn't have enough proof."

"You're just doing your job," Jess said.

"I never saw anyone draw that fast," Rocher declared. "Jess, you were firin' before his gun cleared the holster. And I hear ole Red is plenty fast himself."

"Nothin' to brag about," Clinton said.

"The marshal's right," Jess agreed. "All I did was make a deadly enemy."

"And heat things up between the Colbys and Hatchers," Sam added. "You figure there's goin' to be a war, Marshal?"

"I'll tell you this," Clinton said. "The Hatchers just ain't honorable men. When they make their move, it sure won't be with any warnin'."

"They got a lot to lose," Jess said. "On both sides."

Clinton nodded. "Those two old men, Bull and Lance, they hate each other's guts. They won't be rational. And it's all over free grass."

"And rustling," Jess reminded him.

"So Colby says, but I ain't seen no proof."

"We'll get it now," Sam assured him. "Red Hatcher has to save face with his kinfolk by haulin' in a few more head of Colby beef."

Clinton shrugged and was about to move down the sidewalk when the sound of the lively piano and some laughter drifted from the Hatchers' saloon some twenty feet away. He turned to Jess. "You and your brother sure set yourselves up for a back shootin' with that Texas story. Watch yourselves."

Leading their horses, Jess and Sam walked with Rocher in the moonlight, passing the other saloons in silence. Finally Rocher spoke:

"I did learn a few things workin' at the livery. That Neal Colby, he's been playin' footsies with one of the Hatcher women. That means he could've done some ridin' with the Hatchers. His old man would tan his hide if he found out about it. I figure that's why Neal keeps puttin' on a show about hatin' the Hatchers."

"Thanks." Jess mulled that over.

"Another thing I heard," Rocher added. "That Ed Grange don't never get no mail."

"That's mighty interesting," Jess said.

They crossed back over the bridge. The marshal was far ahead, checking doors.

"Let's take a look at the Colby hangout," Jess suggested.

Rocher laughed. "Ain't you had enough for one night?"

"Reminds me," Jess said. "You're pretty handy to have around in a fight."

"Thanks." Rocher reset his glasses. "And I never even lost my new spectacles. I could even see who I was hittin'."

As they neared the newspaper office, Rocher

decided that he wasn't needed, and he headed for the livery and bed. As Jess and Sam mounted, they could see the lawman ahead, checking doors of the various establishments. Walking back, he looked up at the brothers.

"Sure glad you're calling it a night."

"We're going to stop at the Colbys' saloon," Jess told him.

Clinton frowned and continued on his way.

After riding to the saloon at the end of the street, the brothers dismounted and loosely tied their horses to the hitching rail.

At the smoky window, they peered at the twenty or so Colby cowhands inside. Neal Colby was at the bar. There were a few miners and townspeople. Card games were flourishing. There were no women. The place looked respectable.

"Clinton could be right," Sam said. "Maybe we stirred up enough trouble for one evenin'."

"I'm mighty tired of waiting around for someone to show his hand. We gotta get the word out, but the best thing we can do is find that silver locket and music box."

"How? By ridin' into the Hatcher camp?"

"Now that might work," Jess said.

"I got you figured, Jess, for bein' the most cantankerous fellow I ever met. You sure like to put your foot in it."

Jess only grinned as they entered the saloon. And Sam prepared himself for more trouble.

Chapter Seven

IN the Colby's hangout that Saturday night, Jess and Sam moved over to the bar where Neal Colby was drinking a beer. The brothers ordered more apple cider. Neal snickered.

"Big, tough Darringers," he said.

Jess smiled at him. "Maybe you can help us out, Neal. The reason we rode to Buzzard's Creek might interest you."

"Nothin' you say could interest me."

"Back in July, four or five men rode through Texas and killed a woman near Austin. We're looking for those men. Aim to see 'em hanged."

Neal's face went hard. His eyes narrowed, his mouth tightened. Color hit his wide cheeks. "So what?" he said, turning to stare into the big mirror behind the bar.

"Where were you last July?" Jess asked.

"Go hang yourself." Neal downed his beer. "I got no time to talk to the likes of you." He

115

turned and headed through the tables to the swinging doors.

The saloon continued with its noise and smoke. Jess and Sam finished their cider and returned to their horses and mounted.

"I reckon we've got to throw in a little more ante," Jess said as they rode toward the wagon road. "It's time I told Lorena about the locket and music box."

"You figure Neal gave her one of 'em?"

Jess shrugged. He didn't know anything, but if Neal was in love with Lorena, there was a good chance that he gave presents to her. And if one of the presents was a music box that played "Shenandoah," it would place Neal in Texas. But they just couldn't be that lucky.

After a restless night's sleep, Jess was up early. After breakfast, he and Sam rode two broncs for Gibbs. Some of the men who had not had a bad night were at the fence, waiting for them to be bucked off. Sam took one tumble. Jess stayed in the saddle.

When that was finished around midmorning, Sam sat around with the men telling stories. It was a warm day, and the air was fresh and clean. Lance Colby brought Jess the signed bill of sale for his new mount. As they shook hands, Jess was beaming.

After Colby left, Jess headed for the corral and Comanche. The stallion greeted him with a tossing head and a buck. Jess laughed, then entered the corral to feed and groom him.

"You're a little fat, old friend," he said afterward. "I figure it's time we went for a mighty long ride."

"If I wasn't going to church, I'd go with you."

He turned at the sound of Lorena's voice. She was approaching the fence, her golden hair shining in the morning sun. In a yellow dress with heaps of lace, she was beautiful. Her dark blue eyes were open wide and glistening.

He came to the railing, the stallion nuzzling his back.

"Good morning," he said.

"Would you take me riding one day?"

"Sam and I are looking for rustlers. Wouldn't be safe for you."

"You're a very difficult man, Mr. Darringer."

She was smiling all the while, right into Jess's gut. To chill the warmth she was building in him, he had to get to his main purpose for being here.

"Remember what I told you about the murdered girl in Texas?" he asked. "What I didn't tell you was what the killers took when they left—a silver locket with the initials S.C. and a music box that played 'Shenandoah.'"

Lorena gazed at him strangely. She seemed

flustered. "Why are you telling me all this?" she asked.

"Because one of the men had a receipt from Morley's saddlery made out to a Colby. It was found with her body."

Lorena stiffened, and her eyes flashed hostility. "I told you—stay away from my family."

"The family that robbed you of your gold mine?"

"The family that took me in and raised me like one of their own. Lance Colby has spent more on making me happy than ever was found in that mine."

"And Neal Colby's in love with you. Are you in love with him? Or is Ed Grange your ticket out of here to the big cities?"

"Jess Darringer, if you're picking a fight, you sure are finding one," she said, her face reddening.

"You're right, Miss Lorena, I was trying to rile you. Just looking for information, that's all."

"A little more personal than that," she said.

Jess sobered, realizing she was right. "Then I apologize."

He looked past her as a rider came over the hill. It was Clinton on his big roan, with Sam trailing on foot. Lorena turned to follow Jess's gaze.

The lawman rode up but didn't dismount.

He leaned on the big horn and looked straight at Jess.

"Got some bad news for you. Rocher was found behind the livery this morning, shot in the back."

Jess's sudden anger clouded his face. "And no one heard the shot?" he asked.

"It was Saturday night. The men sleeping in the livery paid no heed. Potter doesn't even care."

"Hatchers," Jess growled. "I'm thinkin' I'm going to take a ride to their spread."

"You got no proof," Clinton said.

"I'm sick and tired of waitin' for your proof."

"They'll shoot you on sight. And if you take the law in your own hands, I gotta arrest you."

"All I'm gonna do is ride over to Hatchers' and find out if they did it. I have a right to defend myself."

Clinton straightened. "You're the most obstinate man I've ever met."

"You tell 'im, Marshal," Sam agreed.

"The marshal's right," Lorena said. "If you ride into the Hatcher place, you'll be shot. If you were a prudent man, you'd wait for the marshal to investigate. But from what I've seen, Mr. Darringer, you have no patience at all."

Jess turned to stroke the stallion's neck. He

knew they were right, but he wasn't going to let Rocher die for nothing.

"Comanche," he said, "I think we'll take a ride. I'll bet there's not a horse in Colorado can catch you."

"A bullet's faster than any horse," Clinton reminded him.

Lorena looked as if she wanted to say something but couldn't. Sam came over to her side and tipped his hat.

"Don't worry, ma'am. Jess is the most peaceable man in our family."

"But he has no sense," Lorena said. "Well, if he's going, so am I."

"No, you're not," Jess said.

"Why would they shoot you down if I'm with you?" she demanded.

"You're not going," he said, "and that's final."

Drawing a deep breath, she scowled and scurried up the hill, lifting her skirts above the grass. Sam was grinning.

"She's got you on the run, Jess."

Clinton wasn't amused. "At least take some men with you."

"And start a war?" Jess asked. "No, thanks."

Disgusted, Clinton turned and rode back over the hill. Sam and Jess started a discussion in which Jess argued Sam was to stay on the ranch.

But an hour later Sam and Jess were heading for town. Jess kept looking over his shoulder, but there was no sign of Lorena. Comanche felt strong and aching to move.

They rode through town and over the bridge, heading for the south hills. It was still warm, but the wind was rising. Dark clouds lined the northwestern horizon.

"This is foolhardy," Sam said. "We're really asking to be shot in the back."

They rounded another hill and sighted some distant cattle in the shade of some trees. As they neared, watching for riders, Jess spoke quietly.

"Wonder how many show signs of a runnin' iron."

"Well, if Colby's brand is a crooked C, how can they change it?"

"Hatchers use a lazy H. A few touches, they can make a crooked C into their own mark by makin' it a larger brand."

As they neared the alerted cattle, they saw a rider coming over the far hill. The nervous steers suddenly bolted and headed for the wash.

The rider was one of the Hatcher sons. He was backed up by six men who came over the hill behind him. Hatcher had an ugly look on his mustached face. Rifle in hand, he reined up near them.

"I'm Sid Hatcher and you fellas are lost," he said to Jess.

"Since you Hatchers have been kind enough to visit our spread, we figured we'd return the favor."

"Now, that just makes me so happy I can't spit," Hatcher said.

"We'd like to see your pa," Jess told him.

The youth sat on his prancing horse with his rifle aimed at them. He wasn't certain what to do. He couldn't look cowardly to his men. He had to take some kind of action.

"We'll take you there," he said. "But don't you try anything. Maybe you oughta hand over those six-guns."

"Not a chance," Jess said.

"Well, I reckon you're so outnumbered it don't matter. You ride on ahead."

"I'd as soon turn my back on a sidewinder."

There was a long, tense moment. Then Hatcher laughed and rode ahead with his men. Some of them looked nervously over their shoulders.

More cattle appeared in the hills and valleys. There was still a lot of grass. It seemed that the Hatchers were short on cattle, all right. Other riders could be seen on a far ridge to the right. Overhead, a pair of buzzards were circling.

As they rounded another hill, the Darringers saw a ranch house, two smaller houses with children playing in front, and sheds and corrals spread along a long rise with scrub pine.

The ranch house was old, leaning, and huge. Smoke was trailing from two chimneys. Several men were in the corrals to their right, working horses.

"I count twenty-four, so far," Jess murmured.

Sam nodded. "And six sons, and Bull."

As they approached, a young woman came out on the porch. A small boy of maybe six was playing near her. She was probably about twenty, with long brown hair that blew in the breeze. She wore a simple print dress and looked rather pretty. She was also wearing a very shiny silver locket.

"Don't you be lookin'," Sid Hatcher growled as they all reined up. "That's my sister."

They dismounted and moved toward the porch.

"Auralie," Sid said, "get back in the house."

She stuck her nose up at him and retreated into the building. Sam was plenty nervous, but Jess walked right up and inside the front door. Sam and young Hatcher followed.

Seated by a huge stone hearth in a large room full of saddles and gear was Bull Hatcher. He was in a chair trimmed with horns. A fire was blazing hot and sparkling.

There were two couches and several chairs, but he was the only one in sight. Rising slightly, he glared at the Darringers. "What are you doing here?" he demanded.

"We came to find out," Jess said, "if you know who shot our friend Rocher in the back."

"We don't need to shoot anyone in the back," Sid snarled. "In fact, now I seen you draw, I can take you any day."

"Lay off," Bull said to his son.

"Rocher was the one who picked you up and threw you a few times last night," Jess told Bull. "Maybe you didn't figure that was a fair fight."

"I don't get even by back-shootin'," Bull said. "When I make a move, you'll know it. So will everyone from here to Denver."

Auralie appeared in a doorway. As she looked at the Darringers, Jess walked across the room to her.

"Mighty pretty locket," he said. "Mind if I see it?"

"She minds," Sid growled. "I told you to stay away from my sister."

Jess ignored him and put his hand forward. She moved closer to him, her dark eyes twinkling. He took up the locket. On the back, a knife had scraped away the silver, but still visible were the letters S.C.

Jess took the locket in his fist and jerked it to break the chain. She gasped. Jess turned to see the Hatchers ready to charge. Bull had risen, his face red with anger. Sid had his hand on his holster. So did Sam.

Jess held out the locket, its chain dangling.

"The initials are S.C.," he told Bull. "Whoever gave this to your daughter was mighty careless when he tried to scrape them off."

"Talk fast or you're a dead man," Bull said fiercely.

"S.C.," Jess said. "Sue Ellen Cambridge, the woman who was murdered in Texas last July."

Slowly, Jess turned his back on them and looked at the frightened woman. "Who gave you this?"

In a panic, she backed against the wall and shook her head.

"Four or five men," Jess said to her. "They came to a woman's house at night. She was all alone. When they left, she was dead. One of the things they took was this locket."

"S.C. could stand for anyone," Sid told him.

"Who gave you this?" Jess repeated.

She resumed shaking her head. Bull Thatcher came over to them. He looked Jess up and down, then turned to his daughter.

"It's all right," he said. "Who gave it to you?"

Tears came to her eyes. "It was Red."

Bull's face turned from red to purple. He walked to the wall and slammed his fist into it. He turned around, steaming and furious.

"Get off my land," he said to Jess.

"The marshal's gonna be payin' you a visit," Jess replied.

"She's not right in the head," Sid told them.

"Who else was in Texas last July?" Jess asked Bull. "How many of your sons were there?"

"My son didn't kill any woman," Bull growled. "Red probably bought that locket from some passin' stranger."

Jess turned to look at the woman. "Did he give you a music box?"

She shook her head, surprised. Jess and Sam moved toward the door, watching the Hatchers. Sam went out first. Jess turned, looking them over.

"I'll tell you one time," Jess said. "I loved the woman they murdered. I'll see them all hang."

Outside, the brothers mounted their horses. The men who had ridden with Sid were nearby, sitting on the ground and watching.

Comanche tossed his head as Jess reined him about. The brothers rode side by side, holding their breath. It seemed an eternity before they were over the hill and out of sight of the ranch house.

"Let's get out of here," Sam said.

They set their horses to full gallop. Any minute, bullets could slam into their backs. Sweat on their faces and bodies, they rode like the wind.

Comanche was faster than Sam's sorrel, so Jess had to hold him back. Over the last hill before town, they reined up and turned in the saddle to look back.

"They'll come after us," Sam said.

"Maybe."

"That old man isn't about to let you hang his son."

Jess led the way down the hillside, past the smelter, and down around the old hotel to the street. Moving up toward the bridge, he looked back. There was still no sign of any riders.

Inside his office, Clinton was sitting with his feet on his desk, sound asleep. As Jess slammed the door, Clinton nearly fell out of his chair. He scrambled for balance and reached for his six-gun.

"Here's your evidence," Jess said, walking up to the desk and laying the locket in front of him. "A music box and this were taken when they killed her. They didn't do a good job of scraping off the initials—S.C., for Sue Ellen Cambridge."

"Where'd you get it?"

"At the Hatchers' place."

Sam added as the brothers sat down in front of the desk, "We rode right into the lion's den, and Jess walks right up to Bull's daughter,

Auralie, and takes it off her neck. She says she got it from Red."

"Enough evidence?" Jess asked.

Clinton leaned back, thoughtful. "Maybe. But you gotta realize, when she's on the stand, she may not admit where she got it. And Red is gonna say he bought it from someone else."

"But someone's gotta know if Red was in Texas in July," Sam argued.

Clinton drummed his fingers, considering.

"Well?" Jess asked.

"It'd take an army to arrest them boys."

"Let's start with Red," Jess said.

"There's another problem," Clinton told them. "Jurisdiction. I reckon we can arrest him all right, but you can't try 'im here. Someone's gotta come up from Texas and get him."

"You got a judge in this town?"

"We got a local justice of the peace for weddings and such. But we also got a circuit judge comes through once a month. He's due on Saturday's stage."

"So he could put Red in jail till the Rangers get up here?" Jess asked.

"Maybe, but ain't no way we could keep Red in jail that long. Bull Hatcher would tear the place apart. We'd have to get him out o' here, maybe to Pueblo or some place south o' here."

"Are you gonna arrest Red?"

"As I see it, the locket's not enough. You gotta put Red down in Texas in July," Clinton said. "You got no witnesses to say that. And there'll be a dozen Hatchers sayin' he never left town. You hold off till I talk with the circuit judge. If he figures there's enough for a warrant, I'll arrest him. If I live through it, that is."

Jess was reddening in his frustration. He drew a deep breath, then rose from his chair. "What about Rocher?"

"See the barber. He's buryin' him this afternoon."

Jess stormed out, leaving the locket with the lawman for safekeeping.

After the burial Jess was calmer. He and Sam decided to eat at the hotel, as it was already sundown. There was Grange and his sister, seated at the long center table with Mr. and Mrs. Colby, who he had learned were spending the night in town. Lorena and Neal would be at the ranch alone. Elizabeth was flirting, as usual.

"Sit with us," Lance Colby invited.

"No, thanks," Jess said, looking straight at Grange. He and Sam walked over to a far corner table. They ordered steak and beans. Outside, the night reflected their faces in the window.

Then he saw Elizabeth's reflection. As she sat down with them, Jess looked at her, pretty in her blue velvet dress. He was in no mood for flirtation, but she looked serious.

"Was the man who was shot your friend?" she asked.

"Rocher was a good man," Jess replied, nodding.

"It seems that Buzzard's Creek has not been a very friendly place for you," she said.

"Tell me, who's handling all this money your brother is collecting?"

"The express office. It's the only bank. Why do you ask?"

"Does your brother have money of his own? Does he have land somewhere? What's he got to offer Lorena Colby?"

"Why, I declare," she said, annoyed. "It seems like you're protecting her."

"Lance Colby has been good to me. I'd take it unkindly if your brother left town with the money."

"That's a terrible thing to say."

"What's more, I can't figure a town this small raisin' the amount of cash needed for a railroad spur. They could hardly get together enough for a month's payroll."

"Mr. Darringer, you are a terrible man," she said, her face red. She stalked back to the long table.

Sam shook his head as he spoke: "Now I can see why you never got married."

Jess shrugged. "Maybe I shouldn't have taken things out on her."

"You gonna go over and apologize?"

"No, I'm not."

After their meal, they rode back along the trail. Anger still boiled in Jess. At the ranch, the brothers separated as Jess turned over the hill to put Comanche in his corral.

It was dark now. Clouds blocked the moon, but the stars were still sprinkled in the sky here and there. It was cold as he unsaddled the stallion.

Rubbing the animal down, he talked out his frustration:

"I know Red Hatcher is one of the killers. I know he gave that locket to his sister."

Jess checked the water and feed, then left the stall. Outside, at the fence, stood Lorena Colby in a heavy black coat.

"Didn't they teach you anything at finishing school?" he said, climbing onto the fence.

"Like what?"

"For one thing, not to sneak up on a man."

"What else?" she persisted, smiling.

"To wear your hair done up in curls or something. When it's free like that, it—"

"Yes?"

He sat on the top railing and looked down at her. She was beautiful. Her blue eyes were dark and glistening. Her pretty lips were parted. She was hugging her coat to her.

More than anything, he wanted to jump down and kiss her, but he fought the temptation, because he was also boiling with anger and frustration.

"Did you tell anyone I'm here lookin' for those killers?" he asked.

"No."

"Why not?"

"You asked me not to. Besides, I knew that no Colby could be involved. And I didn't want you sent away."

Jess didn't grasp her meaning. He was too grim. "Your brother Neal at home?"

"No, he's still in town."

"Just you and the maid?"

"She's asleep. Why?"

"Then I figure it's time you showed me that music box."

"I don't have it."

"You sure acted like it when I asked you before."

"You're wrong," she said, but she was trembling.

He jumped down, grabbed her arm, and marched her up the hill. She struggled, fighting his hard grip, but he was determined to find some answers and maybe some evidence. He was mighty tired of the long wait.

"Jess, you're out of your mind! Let me go!"

"I'm not going to hurt you, but you're gonna show me your room."

"If you take me there, my father will kill you!"

"I told you, I'm not going to hurt you!"

He marched her all the way to the porch and, inside, down the hallway and across the bright lights of the parlor to the foot of the winding stairs.

"All right," she said, tears in her eyes. "Please stop. I'll get it for you."

He hesitated, then decided he could trust her. After freeing her arm, he watched her slowly ascend the stairs. She could lock her bedroom door and wait him out, but he sensed she would not do that.

And he was right. Within minutes, she was at the head of the stairs, carrying a small, decorated wooden box maybe two inches by three. Slowly, she came down the steps, her face white and strained. Tears were trickling down her cheeks.

Jess took the music box as she came to the foot of the stairs. He lifted the lid. It was already cranked up, and the slow, wistful tune of "Shenandoah" came tinkling forth. He closed the lid and looked at her.

"All right," she said. "Neal gave it to me. But that doesn't prove anything."

"Was he in Texas in July?"

"No, he took some cattle down to Santa Fe. Jess, he could have bought that music box from anyone. It may not even be hers. She couldn't have owned the only one, you know."

He handed it back to her, knowing she was right. He was shaken clear to his boots. He had two leads and couldn't prove anything. Sue Ellen Cambridge was dead, but her killers could go free.

He turned round to hide the sudden tears in his eyes. For the first time, he felt he would never find justice for the woman he had once loved. He walked to the hallway and out the front door.

"Jess, wait!"

He stopped without turning. Lorena came to his side and looked up at him. She put a hand on his arm.

"Jess, I'm so sorry," she said softly.

He started to move forward, but she rushed in front of him, put her hand on his cheek. Her touch was shattering, and before he knew it, his arms were around her. She felt wonderful. His right hand moved to crunch the silken softness of her hair.

Standing on her tiptoes, she lifted her lips toward his. Unable to stop himself, he bent his head and kissed her gently. Then he crushed her to him, her face on his chest as he held her tightly. Her free arm slid around his broad back.

He held her on the porch in the darkness. Light from the hall lamps filtered out to them.

His anger and frustration were slowly ebbing. They were being replaced by the realization that he wanted to keep holding her and never stop.

Slowly he forced himself to take her by the arms and push her gently back so that he could look at her face. Tears were still trickling down her cheeks.

"I'm sorry if I was rough on you," he said.

Then, hearing running footsteps, Jess released her, and they turned to watch Neal springing up the porch steps. He looked hot with anger as he stopped to catch his breath. His hand was on his holster.

"Get away from her!" he snarled.

"Neal, it's all right," Lorena told him.

"When Pa finds out you and him were alone in the house, he'll kill him."

She held up the music box. "You gave me this when you came back from Santa Fe. Where did you get it?"

"What difference does it make?" he snapped.

"A girl was murdered in Texas," she said. "A box like this was taken from her."

"Well, I got that down in Alamosa, off a peddler."

Jess felt slammed and hit and burdened. He still believed that Neal was involved, but he couldn't prove it. At this point he couldn't prove anything for certain against Red. He felt a failure, and anger rose up hot within him.

Without looking at Lorena, he charged down the steps, his face burning.

It was a rough night for him. He went to sleep with the memory of Lorena's kiss, but he tossed and turned in anguish.

The rest of the week was the same. Jess didn't see Lorena except from a distance. It was just as well. Not only had her father already warned him that he was no candidate for her hand, but Jess still yearned for his freedom.

On Thursday night he was coming back from Comanche's corral when he saw Sam and Hooper coming out of the bunkhouse. They met at the foot of the hill. Sam was excited.

"Go ahead, Hooper—tell him what you just told me."

"Well, I was up on the ridge when I saw this campfire. I went lookin' because old Kansas is missing. I got close enough to see some of our cattle and two Hatchers. I never did find Kansas."

"Can you take us there?" Jess asked.

"Yeah. Do you want some of the men?"

"No, just the three of us. Are you any kind of a shot?"

"I can knock a squirrel's eye out at ninety feet."

Jess went back for Comanche. The Colbys were all inside the house. He saddled and rode the stallion back over to the other corrals, where Sam and Hooper were ready and mounted.

Jess felt like he was holding his breath all the way in the dark. This was their first chance to catch the rustlers. Their first chance at the Hatchers.

Chapter Eight

In the moonlight Jess, Sam, and Hooper rode over the Colby hills toward the ridge that lined the first rise of the mesa. When they reached the ridge top, it was probably two hours before dawn. Clouds were moving in the black sky. They started north, with Hooper pointing the way. There were clusters of pines and great rocks. The air was cold, cutting to the bone. Jess and Sam drew their jackets more tightly about them. It smelled like rain. They rode another hour before Hooper reined up and pointed to the tiny glow in the distance.

"That's their campfire."

"All right," Jess said. "You go on back."

"Wait for me," a muffled voice called.

Immediately, the three men dismounted, and Jess and Sam crawled down into a deep ravine, following the groans of Kansas, who kept calling the way. Hooper stayed above to keep watch.

Kansas had been shot in the chest and didn't

138

look good. They carried him out of the ravine and laid him on the ground.

"It was Red Hatcher," Kansas muttered. "I caught 'im roundin' up some of our beef. Red just turned around and shot me. I played dead, and he rolled me into the ravine. My horse ran off down that gully."

They found his horse down by a spring, brought it back, and tied him into the saddle. As Hooper led the older man's horse back toward the ranch, Jess and Sam moved forward on their own, leading their mounts and staying as quiet as possible.

It was an hour before dawn. The clouds covered the moon and would not allow early light. The stars were their only guide as they moved through the rocks and trees. When they were near enough, they left the horses tied to the brush and kept going.

They moved into position and looked down at the small clearing where the Hatchers sat by their fire. A running iron was propped up nearby. The camp would have been impossible to spot from any direction but that from which Jess and Sam had come.

It was Red, all right, dealing the cards, his right hand still bandaged. The other brother was Sid, probably still hot from his run-in with Jess at the Hatcher ranch.

An improvised rope corral in the back of the clearing held their horses and three head of cattle. Jess signaled to Sam to stay where he was. Then he continued around the clearing, avoiding the slightest branch or stone.

"You cheated," Red was saying.

"You're a mighty poor loser. And I still say we gotta get off this ridge."

"And have every Colby on us? No, we'll do like before. We'll pick up a few more head, brand 'em, then move back across the mesa and down where we can ford the creek and cut over to our land. Works every time."

"Yeah, but I got me a funny feelin'."

"You know, Sid, sometimes I wonder if you're a girl."

"You'd better grin when you say that."

Red laughed as he shuffled the cards. "Besides," he said, "ain't no grass this part of the mesa, so their hands ain't likely to come this way. All we gotta do is keep pickin' up strays."

"Well, we oughta butcher the last one you branded. You sure messed it up. An oversized brand is one thing, but you smeared it."

"If you think you're so smart," Red said, "then you do the next ones. Show me how good you are."

Red was dealing the cards now. They were sitting Indian fashion near the fire, comfortable in their hideaway. Jess moved near the horses and steers. Six-gun in hand, he was ready, and he hoped that Sam was. Quickly, he stood up and stepped into the firelight.

"Get your hands up! Fast!"

The Hatchers scrambled to their feet, hands in the air. Red was sneering, his hands wavering, looking for a sign of weakness.

"With your left hands, unbuckle them belts!"

"Go ahead, shoot," Red snickered.

"My turn, Jess," Sam said from behind them. "Let me plug 'em this time."

Red stiffened. Finally, the Hatchers unbuckled their gun belts and let them slide to the ground.

"Now the knife in your boot," Jess said to Red. "With your left hand. And you'd better be mighty careful. This Colt has a hair trigger."

"You got nothin' on us," Red snarled. "Them cattle got our brand."

"I know," Jess said. "I can see the iron you used."

"You won't get very far with us," Sid muttered.

"I'm takin' you to town," Jess told them. "If Kansas doesn't make it, you're both gonna hang."

The Hatchers looked startled. They were angry when Sam tied their hands behind their backs.

"We can't ride like this," Red protested.

"You either get up in the saddle or you'll ride belly down," Jess advised him.

"You're dead meat, and you know that!" Red snarled.

"You'll never hold us," Sid warned.

"All we gotta do is hold you till Saturday," Jess told them. "That's when the circuit judge comes through."

So it was that as daylight broke, the Hatchers were pushed and half lifted into their saddles. Their mounts were prancing nervously. Jess put the reins in the Hatchers' teeth. That not only kept them busy but quiet.

With the Hatchers and the cattle, Jess and Sam started back along the ridge, riding until they found the trail down to the hills. By noon they were in sight of the ranch. Clouds had filled the sky, and it was sprinkling already. As they came alongside the bunkhouse, Jess called out for Hooper. Comanche jumped but kept walking.

Two men came out of the bunkhouse. One was Hooper.

"We got Kansas to the doctor in town," he said. "Not sure he'll make it. Mr. Colby's pretty mad about it."

"Get your horse," Jess said. "We could use a hand with the cattle here. And drag out our slickers."

He turned in the saddle as Hooper hurried to the corral. Red and Sid were looking plenty mean, but not half as dangerous as Bull Hatcher was going to be.

Glancing up the hill, Jess saw Lance Colby and Lorena hurrying toward them.

"I'm going with you," Colby told him.

"So am I," Lorena said.

They set out for town. All were wearing their slickers, including the prisoners. It was sprinkling just enough to wet the dust and worry them.

Entering town, they headed through the usual wagons and mules and horses. People gathered on the sidewalks and stared. A small boy ran down the boardwalk to the jail.

As they neared his office, Clinton came out holding his shotgun. The Hatchers were pulled down without ceremony, and Clinton took charge. He sent Hooper down to the livery with two other citizens to secure the cattle as evidence. Hooper also took the Darringers' horses with him to find stalls.

Then Clinton marched the prisoners inside and locked them in separate cells. Only then did he untie them through the bars. The prisoners jerked off their slickers and cursed under their breath.

Clinton sat down at his desk to preside over the group. He looked mighty pleased as he leaned back in his chair, fingertips together. His visitors removed their slickers. Lorena and her father sat facing him. Jess and Sam stood.

"You figure you got enough evidence now?" Jess asked dryly.

Clinton nodded, fighting a grin. "You got 'em at the scene all right. You got the runnin' iron and the cattle, and you got Kansas, who already gave me a signed statement of what happened, and he gave it in front of witnesses."

"How is he?" Colby asked. "I gotta see him."

"Not good," Clinton said. "The circuit judge doesn't get here until tomorrow, and it's not going to be easy holding off Bull Hatcher."

"I'll bring you all the men you want," Colby told him. "You can deputize 'em."

"There are only two men you got who would be of any help," Clinton said. "They're right here."

"All right," Colby said, "but I'm still sendin' a few boys into town. And I'll bunk in here."

Lorena looked distressed, afraid for her father. Clinton leaned back in his chair and shook his head.

"No, Lance, I'd rather have you out on the street where you could do more good in a showdown. I know you'd be mighty careful of the innocent citizens out there."

"I'll get a room at the hotel," Colby said. "You get some fellas to watch the cattle. I'll send Hooper back to the ranch with my daughter. He'll send Neal and three other men, just in case."

"I'm staying," Lorena said. "You may as

well get me a room. Mother can send me what I need."

Colby gave a reluctant grunt, obviously used to his daughter's stubborn ways.

"Bull's particularly fond of you," Clinton said to Jess. "I mean after you and your brother rode right into their camp and faced 'em down at their ranch."

Colby was grinning. "I heard about that."

"Had nothin' to do with the rustlin'," Jess said. "It was personal."

Lorena stood up, glanced shyly at Jess, and then left with her father. Jess and Sam sat down in the two chairs while the marshal put his feet on his desk.

"All right, Jess," Clinton said. "You've got step one—the evidence. Now you tell me how we're gonna keep Bull Hatcher out of this jail."

"We'll have to hole up in here, and get a steel bar for the door. And enough food and coffee and ammunition."

"Won't do you no good," Red called out.

"Lots of water in case of fire," Sam added.

"This old jail has an adobe roof," Clinton told him. "They put it on to keep the place cool. Won't be easy to burn us out, especially if it keeps rainin'. More likely, they'll try to bust in."

"We'd better be set up by tonight," Jess said.

It was agreed that Sam and Jess would take turns going for a meal at the hotel. Jess went first, leaving his slicker behind and dodging the light rain. He visited the doctor's office to see Kansas, but he was sleeping, and the doctor couldn't tell him anything. Then Jess went along to the store to order supplies for the jail.

At the hotel, he saw Grange in the lobby. He still didn't like the man. The Colbys were registering at the desk, and Grange was talking with them.

Elizabeth was coming down the stairs, fresh and cool in a green silk gown. Ignoring the Colbys and her brother, she headed straight for Jess and took his right arm.

"Jess, I was so worried about you. I heard all about how you went to the Hatchers' place. Rode right into their camp. You were so brave."

Colby and Lorena turned, listening and watching.

"And then you caught those rustlers," Elizabeth added, leaning against his arm as she held it. "I'm very proud of you."

Jess looked past her at the strain on Lorena's face. He felt mighty uncomfortable. But he didn't have to worry. Lorena walked toward them and looked sternly at Elizabeth's hand.

"You must be careful of his gun hand," Lorena said.

Elizabeth was embarrassed and withdrew her hand quickly. Grange hurried over to stand between the women.

"Lorena," he said, "is something wrong?"

Caught between the railroad man, who wanted to marry her, and Jess, whom she had lovingly kissed, Lorena hesitated. Her face was turning pink.

"I'm sure Miss Colby is just upset," Elizabeth said, "because there's going to be trouble now that the Hatchers are arrested."

"I'm not afraid," Lorena assured her.

She went back to her father, who had been listening to the conversation with dismay. She took his arm and went up the stairs with him. At the top of the landing, she paused and looked down. Jess had been watching her, and his face turned hot. Then she disappeared.

"She's in love with you," Elizabeth said to Jess.

Grange looked angry. "Nonsense," he told her. "Let's get our rest, Elizabeth. It's too wet out for our walk."

She squeezed Jess's hand before following her brother upstairs. Still dumbfounded, Jess went in to have his meal.

Later that night at the jail, Jess and Sam and the marshal settled in. It was a strange feeling, being sworn in as deputies. The badges felt heavy on the brothers' shirts.

The office was a large rectangle, about twenty feet wide and thirty feet long. The two cells were on the right rear half of the building.

A storage shed had been built in the left rear half, next to the cells, with no inside door.

On the west wall, Clinton's bunk had been pulled forward, beside the stove. His desk sat in the back left corner. Two bunks had been added for the Darringers, set along the east wall. That left a clear path between the cells and the front door. There was no back entrance.

A lamp hung by the door and another was on the desk, both turned low.

"I'll make a fresh pot of coffee," Clinton said.

Jess nodded and continued his assessment of the room. There were shuttered windows on each side of the front door, which was now crossed by a steel bar. The only other windows were in each cell, set about eight feet above the floor and close to the ceiling. They were only four inches high and about eight inches wide, with a bar in the center. On each side wall, about eye level, there were several slits for a rifle barrel. The place was a fortress.

The rain was heavy now, beating at the roof and windows. The wind was rising. They heard lightning crackle in the sky. A chill entered through cracks in the floor. Clinton shoved more wood into the stove.

Along with some blankets, Hooper had thoughtfully brought Jess's squeezebox, and he sat toying with the handle.

"Ain't sure what kind of sentence the judge will hand out," Clinton said. "For rustlin' nowadays, it'll be prison. But if Kansas dies. . . ."

"You don't have to worry," Red called out. "We won't be in here for long. By tomorrow mornin' our pa will be here to get us out."

"Any way to shut them up?" Jess grunted. He placed the concertina on his lap and began to play and sing the sorrowful song of the dying cowboy found in the Streets of Laredo.

As Jess sang, it became quiet in the jail cells. Clinton had his feet on the desk and was dozing. Sam lay on a bunk, listening and keeping time with his fingers.

When Jess finally finished the many verses, he set his squeezebox aside and helped himself to coffee from the stove. Rain and wind pounded the building. He looked around the room at the shuttered windows, the rifle slits, and the steel bar across the front door. Short of dynamite, no one could enter without a fight. And Bull wasn't about to blow up his sons.

As he lay back on his bunk later, with the lamps turned low and Clinton taking the first guard, Jess stared at the shuttered window just beyond his feet. It was going to be a long night.

Chapter Nine

AN hour before dawn on Saturday, there was a knock on the door. On watch and heating the coffee, Jess turned slowly. Clinton and Sam sat up in their bunks.

"It's me—Doc," a voice called.

Sliding the window shutter aside near the front door, Sam peered out, then nodded his okay to Jess.

When Jess opened the door, the old doctor just stood, hunched in his slicker in the light rain, looking distressed and adjusting his spectacles. Finally he spoke.

"Kansas. I lost him. He died in his sleep."

"Thanks for letting us know," Clinton said.

Jess closed and barred the door and glared at the Hatchers, who were sitting up in their cells and listening.

"Now it's murder," Jess said.

"I didn't shoot 'im," Sid called out.

"Don't matter much," Clinton told him.

"You was there, and you both were committin' a felony. It's murder, all right."

"But it wasn't my idea!" Sid shouted.

"Shut up!" Red snapped at him.

Clinton left the windows partly unshuttered, allowing some air to enter. The clouds were breaking up, and a few stars were visible, but no moon. They kept the lamps burning low. Helping himself to some of the strong coffee, he pulled out his pocket watch.

"Breakfast oughta be here shortly."

Soon, about the time the rain stopped, there was a knock on the door, and it was the waiter with a stack of trays of food. And with him was Lorena, still in her riding clothes and a heavy coat.

"Your father know you're here?" Clinton growled.

"He's asleep," she said, entering.

The waiter set the trays on the desk and left. As Clinton served the prisoners by sliding trays under their cell doors, Lorena gave a tray to Sam, who was sitting on his bunk.

Then she turned to Jess. She had a beautiful smile.

"I'm sorry about yesterday, about Elizabeth," she said.

"It's all right," Jess told her, sitting at the desk in one of the front chairs. She sat down next to him as he uncovered his tray and began to eat.

Clinton came to the desk, facing them as he sat down to his breakfast. He was definitely annoyed at her presence.

"It's not even daylight," she said.

"Just the same," Clinton told her, "you get on out of here."

"As soon as I have some of that coffee," she said, rising. She made a face at the cups and finally discovered one that wasn't coated inside. She filled it and sat near Jess once more.

"The stage oughta be in around midday," Clinton said.

"Where will you have this trial?" Jess asked, glancing toward the prisoners.

Clinton shrugged. "Unfortunately, across the creek at the old hotel. They turned the old dining room into an office and a courtroom. That's a mighty long way from here. It'd be headin' right into Hatcher country. Fifty yards from the street to the bridge, and one heck of a long way down to the old hotel."

"Can't you find some place this side of the creek?" Jess asked.

"We'll see what the judge has to say."

"I'll be glad when it's over," Lorena said.

As she slowly stood up, the men rose with her. She glanced shyly at Jess, then headed toward the door.

"Jess, you'd better see her back to the hotel," Clinton said.

Pulling on his jacket and Stetson, Jess

walked ahead of her. Sam checked the window. There was no sign of the Hatchers. Lorena followed Jess outside. It was still dark, but the stars were shining in the clearing sky. The air was damp and cold. As they walked to the boardwalk, she asked softly, "What are you going to do about Neal?"

"I can't prove anything."

"I'm sure he's not involved in that Texas crime."

"Did he ever ride with the Hatchers?" Jess asked.

"No. He hates them."

"Someone said he was seeing a Hatcher woman."

"If you mean Bull's daughter, I understand they keep her a prisoner out there."

"I saw her at the Hatcher ranch. She looked mighty unhappy."

"With Bull for a father, and those terrible brothers, I suppose she is."

"Are you going to marry Ed Grange?"

His question startled him. One kiss of compassion had not given him the right to ask. Besides, a man yearning to wander all his life had no reason to question her.

He was glad it was dark. Wishing he could take the question back, he fell silent. They were on the boardwalk now, heading for the hotel, which was nearby.

"I don't know," she said softly.

At the hotel, she walked slowly up to the porch and turned to gaze down at him. With the lamps burning behind her, he couldn't see her face, only the spun gold of her hair outlined in the light.

"Please be careful," she said.

He nodded, waited until she was safely inside, and then returned to the boardwalk. It was almost dawn now. The sky was red in the east. Looking toward the creek, he saw no movement from the Hatcher side. The buildings were dark. The single street was as empty and abandoned as on the Colby side. Even the miners knew when to be scarce.

Back in the marshal's office, Jess wandered about and then sat on his bunk near the front window. Sam was stretched out, snoozing.

"This judge, how is he, anyway?" Jess asked.

"He's a hanging judge," Clinton said.

"Not anymore," Red called out. "Not after today. My pa won't let nothin' stop him from gettin' us out."

Tired of listening, Jess took up his squeezebox and began to play and sing verses of "I Ride an Old Paint."

"If I couldn't sing any better'n that," Red shouted, "I'd shoot myself."

Suddenly a shot rang outside, and then Sam ran to the window, slid the shutter aside, and peered out into the early light.

"They're here," he said.

Clinton and Jess came over to peer past Sam's shoulder. There were about thirty riders in the street, lined up side by side like cavalry, their rifles pointed skyward. In the middle and riding forward was Bull Hatcher. He looked for all the world like the devil come home to roost.

Clinton moved close to the window and shoved out his shotgun. "That's far enough, Bull!" he shouted.

The big man reined up, his bearded face hot with anger. "Clinton, you got no right to keep my boys in there."

"They was caught red-handed with a runnin' iron and some of Colby's cattle," Clinton said. "What's more, they shot Kansas in cold blood and left him to die. But he lived long enough to get them hanged."

Rising tall in his saddle, Bull appeared ready to explode. His men, including four sons, were tense and ready. "You gonna open up?" he bellowed. "Or do I gotta bust my way in?"

"You take one step closer," Clinton said, "and I'll blast you with this shotgun."

Bull considered the situation. Then he signaled his men to dismount and scatter. He faced the jail once more and demanded, "You gonna let me see my sons, Clinton?"

"You leave your gun belt on the saddle."

Bull swung down, unbuckled his gun belt,

hung it on his saddle horn, and started to walk forward.

"I don't like it," Jess said.

Clinton opened the door for the big man. At that moment, four men charged in with him, having slipped around under the window level. They had weapons out and were aiming wildly.

Jess slammed his fist in one man's face, shoving him against another. Bull jumped to the side as Clinton hit a third with his shotgun butt, full in the face. Then he struck the fourth. Within minutes the four were a bloody mess, kicked and forced out of the jail.

As the door slammed after them, Clinton turned to Bull and said, "I reckon that means I'd better lock you up for trying a jailbreak."

"Now hold on. I didn't know what those boys were gonna do."

"Go ahead and talk to your sons," Clinton told him. "But make it fast."

"Pa!" Red called.

"Get us out o' here!" Sid added.

Both were frantically gripping the bars of the cells.

"No, I see they're all right," Bull said. "Just let me out of here."

Clinton thought for a moment, then slowly unbarred the door. "Don't you be tryin' anything, Bull. I'd make sure your sons went down with me."

"What kind of lawman are you?" Bull growled.

Once the big man was outside, Clinton slammed and barred the door and returned to the window.

"He's not giving up," Jess told him.

"Now he knows the setup," Sam said. "He might try dynamite."

"More likely, he's gonna wait out there and try to get us when we cross over to the court," Clinton replied. "He don't want anything to happen to his sons."

Jess peered out the left front window. There was no sign of the Hatchers, and the street was empty. People were apparently hiding behind closed doors.

"They've scattered," Jess said. "But here comes Colby and three of his sons, and three cowhands."

Jess watched the men as they came from the direction of the livery stable. Suddenly bullets spattered the mud in front of the Colbys as they stepped off the boardwalk. They jumped back, lifting their rifles and dropping their bedrolls.

"We got you covered!" Bull shouted from somewhere. "No one's going in that jail, and no one's comin' out."

The sons and three hands backed off, but Colby stepped forward. Again bullets hit the ground in front of him. He stopped, furious.

"Blast you, Bull Hatcher!" Colby yelled. "I know you're holed up in that hotel. But you ain't scarin' me any. I'm walkin' right into that jail, and you ain't gonna stop me, because that would be cold-blooded murder."

"One step and I cut off your daughter's hair."

Colby froze, and Neal looked stunned. Jess felt his face grow cold and his gut start boiling.

"You're bluffin'!" Colby shouted.

"Just try me!" Bull called back.

"I don't believe it," Colby persisted.

"Well, let me tell you how it was," Bull shouted. "That fancy feller, Grange, he looked at us cross-eyed, but was too scared to spit. We banged 'im up, anyway. He'll tell yuh we got her. You'll probably find him hidin'."

Jess was peering through the rifle slits on the hotel side of the jail. He could see a rifle at a second-story window. He pointed it out to the marshal, who also was looking.

"We'll make a trade," Bull called.

"Show me she's all right."

Then, his fist in Lorena's hair, Bull shoved her partway out the window, its white curtains draped over her face. In a few seconds he jerked her back inside.

Colby was in a quandary. It wasn't just trading his daughter for men who had rustled his cattle. It was against his whole way of life. He had settled this valley and the hills. Fighting

Cheyenne, the land, and the weather, he had survived. But everything he stood for was about one inch high compared to the life of his daughter.

"I got no say," Colby called out.

"Go ahead, talk to the marshal."

Leaving his sons and the men, Colby went to the jail and was allowed to enter. There was sweat on his red face.

"Clinton, we gotta get my daughter out o' there."

"I don't think they'll hurt her," Clinton said.

"I don't want one grimy hand on her."

"No matter what we do," Jess said, "they'll see us make a move. I'm sure some of 'em got into the newspaper office on the other side."

"So what are you suggesting?" Clinton asked.

"We make the trade," Jess said.

"And then what?" Clinton persisted.

"I don't know yet, but we can't leave her in there."

"Bull can't help himself," Colby said. "He has to give his sons a chance. He'll want 'em to have a run for it."

"Don't worry," Jess replied. "No matter what happens, we'll track 'em down."

They sent Colby back outside.

"What's the deal?" Colby called out.

"The bridge," Bull shouted back. "We'll

take her over to the other side. Once we're clear, you bring my boys to the bridge."

"When?"

"Right now."

Colby turned to look at the partly open door. Clinton nodded.

Within a minute, Hatcher men began to appear from all directions, leading their horses. Jess stepped outside with Clinton and Sam, and he watched as Bull and his other four sons came out of the hotel. Lorena was being dragged by two of the sons. She was still in her riding clothes, without her coat, and her long hair was flying about her face. She looked small and helpless as they pulled her down the boardwalk and into the mud, heading for the bridge.

The plank structure was twenty feet long and ten feet wide. It had a single railing, four feet high, on each side. Beneath it in the deep chasm, water raced white and wild, nearly at flood height from the night's rain.

The streets on both sides of the creek were empty except for the Hatchers and Colbys. Hot in the face, Lance Colby watched Jess and Clinton bring out the prisoners. Red and Sid had their hands tied behind their backs with short ropes. Sam was trailing.

The rancher, his angry sons, and the three hands walked ahead of the lawmen, their rifles pointed downward. The Hatchers were all over the bridge now. They spread out on the other side. At the bridge entrance, Bull and Lorena stood, his hand fastened around her right arm. She looked barely able to stand.

East to west on the Hatcher side were six cowhands, Hatcher's four sons, Hatcher and Lorena at the bridge, and another twenty hands lined up west of the structure.

On the Colby side, east to west, stood Lance Colby, Neal, Sam, Jess, and Clinton at the bridge with the prisoners, Hack and Harley with Colby's three hands west of the structure, plus four townsmen who had moved in with rifles to try to even the fight.

Between them, the raging waters were white and six feet deep in the rock-walled chasm. There was no cover for either group of men.

Lorena looked faint, barely able to stand. Bull gripped her arm. Early sunlight was moving into the eastern sky.

"You start my boys," Bull called out. "I'll start your daughter."

Lorena was barely able to stand, but Bull gave her a shove. She reached for the railing. Gripping it, she pulled herself along slowly. Jess and Clinton released their grip on the prisoners, who, still with hands tied behind their backs, started across.

Suddenly the thunder of the incoming stage caught everyone's attention. Six big horses in harness were charging into town from the north side of the creek, yanking along a heavily laden Concord. Everyone turned for a quick look.

Everyone but Lorena. With a bound, she was over the railing and dropping straight into the raging waters. As she disappeared into the white foam, one of Hatcher's sons opened fire at her.

In a fury, Neal fired at him, and the son fired back. Neal doubled up in agony but continued to fire.

Jess and Clinton grabbed Sid and Red from behind, tossed them to the ground, and whipped out their six-guns.

The gunfire was wild from both sides. Men dropped to their bellies and fired across the creek at one another. Six of the Hatcher men threw up their hands, backed away, and took off.

Men were dying on both sides. Bull was screaming and charging across the bridge with his rifle blasting away. Lance Colby rose from the ground and fired, hitting Bull square in the belly. Bull hollered and fell to his knees, clutching his middle.

Hack and Harley were shot dead center. Jess hit two of Hatcher's sons, then made a running jump through rifle fire and leaped into the raging waters to find Lorena.

The force of the water threw him against the banks. He managed to keep his eyes open part of the time, but the current was fierce. Soon he was thrown into a shallower part where the creek widened. He emerged, gasping for air, and then he saw Lorena struggling to get up on the north bank.

He swam to her and fought the icy water as he put his arm around her waist. She was clawing at the mud above. He gave her a shove and she made it. He was barely able to hang on to the side.

Once she was up, she lay flat on her stomach and held out her hand. He caught her small fingers. It was just enough to allow him a good grip on the bank, and he drew himself up.

She had rolled over and was coughing. He got on his knees, pulled out his six-gun, and shook out the water.

"Are you all right?" he asked.

"Yes," she replied, her face in her hands.

He hesitated. There was still rifle fire by the bridge. He started to rise, then paused on one knee.

He reached over, placed a hand on her shoulder, and squeezed it gently. She didn't move or look up.

Jess rose and headed up the creek bank. The firing had stopped. Red and Sid were still prisoners, and Sam and Clinton were marching them back to the jail.

Clinton had been hit in the right shoulder. Hack and Harley were dead. Sam and Lance

Colby had escaped injury. Two of Colby's men lay facedown. Three of the townsmen had been hit, but not seriously.

Except for the six Hatcher men who had retreated to the far street, no one was left standing on the south side. The four sons were dead. Only two men seemed to be able to sit up. Bull lay dead in the middle of the bridge.

Neal was on his back, bleeding from his right side. Colby, with tears in his eyes from the deaths of Harley and Hack, squatted down by Neal.

Kneeling, Jess looked down at Neal's white face. Neal was trying to talk. He looked like he was dying. Worse, he seemed to know he was. Clinton and Sam returned to stand over them.

Finally Neal found his voice. It was hoarse but audible. "Pa, I can't die in sin," he moaned.

"Son," Lance said, "don't talk. The doctor's coming."

But Neal turned his head to gaze up at Jess. He said, "You were right. I met the Hatchers down in Texas. There was Red and Sid, and two cousins who were killed after the holdup in Buzzard's Creek."

"What do you mean?" Colby asked, choking.

"Pa, I left Santa Fe and went to Texas for a lark. Red liked me 'cause I'd been courtin' his sister. So I rode with them. We was all liquored up when we came on that woman's house. I didn't go in. I was curled up asleep, out by the fence." Neal coughed. His eyes glazed as he continued. "Later on, Red gave me the music box, sayin' he bought it from her. I didn't know what they done to get it, not until Darringer made such a fuss. Then, when I asked Red, he just laughed and told me what happened. I ain't slept since."

"Don't try to talk," Colby said. "The doctor's comin' now."

"Tell Lorena," Neal moaned. "Tell her I didn't do nothin' to that woman."

"I believe you," Lorena said tearfully.

Neal stared up at her, lifting a bloody hand. He winced as the doctor kneeled at his side and examined him.

Tears spilled down Lorena's face. Sobbing so that he couldn't talk, Colby stood up and put his arms around her. She buried her face in his chest.

"He'll be all right," the doctor said, working on Neal's wound. "It missed his vital parts."

Colby caught his breath, and Lorena sobbed with relief. Though he realized that he wasn't going to die, Neal seemed relieved that he had told the truth. He grimaced as the doctor worked on him.

"I'm sorry I let you down, Pa," he said in anguish.

"It's all right, son," Colby assured him.

"The way I see it," Jess said, "the only Hatcher left up there is Auralie. Seems like she's going to need a man around to run the place."

Neal gazed at him, grimacing in pain as the doctor tightened the bandage. Then he digested Jess's words, and he managed to smile.

The doctor had moved on, and he was checking for life among the prone men on all sides. Townspeople were coming out now. Women stayed back. Men came forward to help, from both sides of the creek.

On the Hatcher side, including Bull and his sons, twenty-three men had died, two were wounded, and six had backed away. On the Colby side, two hands were dead and one was wounded, and three of the townsmen had been hit. Neal and Clinton had also been hit. Hack and Harley were dead.

Jess looked around at the carnage. He was sick to his stomach. One of Hatcher's sons had fired at Lorena, starting the bloody battle. Jess hated what he saw. This was not what he had expected when he took the trail to find Sue Ellen's killers.

"Clinton, is this what you call law and order?" a booming voice asked.

Everyone turned to see a man of about fifty in a long black coat with a crisp white collar on his new shirt. He had his hands on his gun belt, his coat shoved aside. He had a long, deeply lined face. His nose was almost flat, and his dark, gleaming eyes were fixed on the slaughter.

"Judge," Clinton said to him, "we got two prisoners."

"I sure hope you have more evidence than last time."

"We got 'em for rustlin' and killing a Colby ranch hand. And if that ain't enough, we just got a witness to tie 'em in with the murder of a woman in Texas. We don't need that prosecution at the moment, but there ain't no statute of limitations on murder."

"Well, let's get on with it," the judge said. "The coach leaves in three hours."

When all the dead and wounded had been cared for, court was set up in the old hotel on the Hatcher side. Sid and Red were seated at a table in front of the judge's bench, which was a desk elevated on a platform. Their lawyer was an educated miner who had had experience in court. The defendants pleaded not guilty to rustling and murder. They waived jury trial on the advice of their lawyer, who knew that the evidence against them was staggering.

Even though he was a witness, Jess Darringer was also the prosecutor. He had been pushed into it by Clinton, since Sam's testimony was the same as Jess would have given.

In the rows of chairs, townspeople from both sides of the creek watched and waited. In the first row on Jess's side of the courtroom, Lorena and her father sat together. She looked as if she were in a trance.

In the first row behind the prisoners sat Auralie Hatcher, having been brought in by some of the Hatcher men. She was white-faced, and tears trickled down her cheeks. She had just lost a father and four brothers, and she was soon going to lose Red and Sid. It was obvious that if a trial were ever held in Texas, she would not tell anyone that Red had given her the locket.

Hooper was Jess's first witness, and he began telling his story.

"And where are the three head of cattle?" Jess prompted.

"Down at the livery, under guard."

The running iron was introduced in evidence. A recess was taken for the judge to view the altered brands. Then the doctor and Clinton testified to Kansas's dying statement, that Red had shot him in cold blood. The document was also introduced in evidence.

The Hatcher brothers sat white-faced, gritting their teeth.

Then Sam testified how he and Jess had found Red and Sid at the campfire. "They were bold as brass," he said. "Even talking about

how Red did a bad job on one brand. Sid suggested they butcher that one."

When the prosecution finally rested its case,
the judge turned to the defense lawyer.

"Are you putting on a case for the defense,
Mr. Cox?"

"Well, Your Honor, that depends. If we can
make a deal, then we won't be fightin' this. My
clients don't want to hang. And if they did,
that poor sister of theirs would be left without
any grown kin."

The judge tapped his fingers on his desk. He
looked from the tearful Auralie to Jess.

"Mr. Prosecutor?"

Jess was in turmoil. He could take revenge
for Sue Ellen by watching these men hang. It
would ease his conscience. It would be justice
for Sue Ellen. On the other hand, twenty-seven
men had just died at Buzzard's Creek. He
could still picture the carnage. It made him
sick to remember it.

Jess turned to look at Lance Colby, who only
shrugged. Lorena's dark blue eyes were down-
cast, and tears were on her face. He saw no
hate or thirst for revenge. Nor did he feel any
himself. There had been too much destruction
of human life this day.

With his hand on his leather coat, Jess
thought of the letter in the inside pocket. The
letter from his mother, asking him only to have
the men arrested. He would have to write her

and tell her the conclusion of this trial. What did he want her to read? What was just and fair?

Red and Sid sat with their heads hanging, faces white. Clearing his throat, Jess knew that his mind was made up.

"Your Honor," he said, "a lot of men died today. This valley and town won't be the same because of what happened here this morning."

"Get to the point," the judge growled.

"I'd like to see these men hang," Jess said. "For poor old Kansas and for what they did to a fine lady in Texas. But there's been enough death from this. If they get sent off to prison for life, with no parole ever, then the prosecution will be satisfied."

"That satisfactory, Mr. Cox?" the judge asked.

The miner-lawyer conferred with his clients in whispers. Then he straightened and nodded his assent. And so it was that the judge found the defendants guilty and sentenced them to prison for life, with no possibility of parole. He finished:

"Marshal Clinton, you will transport these men to Canon City."

As court was adjourned, Jess stood behind the small table and watched the crusty old judge leave. The crowd slowly departed from the courtroom. With his right arm in a sling and his shotgun in his left hand, Clinton marched off with the prisoners, Sam assisting.

Jess turned around. Only Colby and Lorena remained.

"I'd take it kindly," Colby said, "if you'd come to my sons' funeral this afternoon."

Jess nodded as they left. He sat in the courtroom and stared at the flags near the back wall. He thought of how far he had come from the day he had read his mother's letter.

Today, frontier justice, however crude the trial, had somehow avenged Sue Ellen. Two of her killers were killed while trying to escape after committing a robbery. The other two were going to prison for life, for killing someone else. Yet it all seemed to fit. Rising and turning to leave, he saw Clinton returning.

"Judge wanted to see me after the trial," Clinton said. "I figure I know why. Maybe you oughta come along, Jess."

They went into the back room that had been set up for the judge's chambers. A big desk was covered with papers. Shelves were stacked with more. Two fat law books were lonesome on the top shelf.

"Marshal," the judge said as they sat in front of his desk, "I brought a warrant for you to serve."

Clinton took the paper from the judge's outstretched hand and read aloud:

" 'The state of Colorado, to the marshal of

Buzzard's Creek: Greeting. You are hereby ordered to arrest Edward Grange, also known as Benson Hardwick, also known as Carl Stoneman, and him safely keep, so that you can later bring him before a court of this state.' "

Jess straightened. He had suspected Grange, but the aliases he used made Jess suddenly wonder about Elizabeth. He couldn't believe she was involved.

"You serve this warrant," the judge said to Clinton, "even though it means holding up the stage for another trial. Then you'll have three prisoners to transport. Will you have help?"

"My first choice would be Jess and Sam Darringer."

"We're movin' on," Jess said, shaking his head.

"I know several good men needin' a grubstake," Clinton said. "I figure they'll jump at it."

"Good," the judge said. "This Grange used to work for the railroad, all right. But he found a way to make more money, collecting from small towns with a promise of a spur. He knew all the right language and even had some fancy railroad stationery. He still had cards showing he was a superintendent."

"Jess," Clinton said, "the judge had written me, but I couldn't say much until I knew if he had enough for a warrant."

"I never liked the man," Jess told him. "What about his sister?"

Clinton shrugged. "We're not sure. It's possible his real name is Grange and she's innocent. But the warrant's only for Ed Grange."

"Mr. Darringer," the judge said, "I must say, despite your family's reputation, that you acted with distinction this day."

"Thank you, Your Honor," Jess said.

Clinton and Jess left the courtroom. As they crossed back over the bridge to the other side, they saw the stage being loaded in front of the hotel.

Grange and his sister were standing on the boardwalk with carpetbags. Clinton, his right arm in a sling, didn't have his shotgun. He hesitated.

"I'll take him," Jess said. "You just serve the warrant."

"Well, you're still deputized, and don't you forget it."

Jess nodded, and advanced along the boardwalk at Clinton's side. He remembered that Grange was supposed to be a fast draw and often practiced along the creek. His face hot, Jess wasn't ready to die. He had too many trails to ride. Yet this man was an unknown.

As Grange saw them coming, his hard face darkened, and his little black mustache curled with his upper lip. It was obvious that he knew what was in store for him.

Walking away from his sister, Grange moved into the street, his coat back from his six-gun.

Chapter Ten

T HE sun was high in the sky at Buzzard's
Creek. The stage was being loaded in front of
the hotel. Elizabeth Grange stood on the
boardwalk with her carpetbag. Next to her
were an elderly man and woman, also ready to
travel.

The street was nearly empty as townspeople
prepared for the afternoon funerals that would
be held at the little white church on the hill behind the livery, as soon as the preacher returned from the Hatcher burial on the south
side of the creek.

Elizabeth watched her brother walk into the
street. She turned and saw Clinton and Jess
coming up the boardwalk. As Jess moved into
the street, she became frightened.

Clinton paused some twenty feet away on
the boardwalk. Jess stood opposite him. Clinton drew the warrant out of his pocket. Three
men and a woman, coming up near him, suddenly veered aside and headed for the hotel.

The couple standing next to Elizabeth turned abruptly and also headed for the hotel. Setting her bag down, Elizabeth came to the back of the stage to see what was going on. Her face white, she looked from her brother to Jess. Both were standing in the mud, their right hands at their sides.

"Ed," she said anxiously.

"Get back, Elizabeth," Grange snapped.

Slowly, she backed away toward the hotel. Her dark eyes were wide, and her gloved hand rose to her throat. She backed up the steps to the railing and grasped it. Others stood and watched in the hotel entrance.

Lorena and her father appeared on the porch and stared.

"Grange," Clinton called, "I have a warrant for your arrest."

"On what charge?" Grange demanded to know.

"Lying to the citizens of Buzzard's Creek," Clinton said. "Taking their money under false pretenses. You don't work for the Denver and Rio Grande. Not anymore."

"The money's in the bank," Grange said.

"No," a man called from the porch. "Marshal, he drew it out this mornin'. Said he was takin' it to General Palmer, figurin' it would show our good faith and maybe the general would go ahead and put in the spur."

Grange's face was grim. "Go ahead, Clinton, serve your warrant—if you dare," he snarled, his grand pose giving way to grim defiance.

"My deputy will serve it for me," Clinton said.

"Darringer?" Grange laughed.

Jess studied the man, who didn't appear afraid. Grange was an unknown, a possible fast gun. Although Jess was swift with his six-gun, he didn't practice daily. In fact, that was something he usually did only in the winter on his wanderings. He suddenly felt unprepared.

Worse, he was thinking how he didn't want to die. He was remembering his mother's sweet face, the brothers he wanted to see again, Sam, whom he was just getting to know, and most of all, the golden-haired young woman on the hotel steps. He knew he was asking for trouble now. He was hungry to live, and gunfighters had to think only of the moment.

With sweat on his back, Jess stood watching the man, waiting for a sign. He saw Grange's face crinkle under his eyes.

It was then that Grange drew, his gun fast in his hand. But Jess was faster, firing before Grange could pull the trigger. The bullet slammed into Grange's chest and knocked him backward. Grange stared at him, trying to lift his gun.

Elizabeth screamed. Grange took a step forward. There was blood on his shirt. He snarled and dropped to his knees.

"Blast you, Darringer!" he cried.

Again Grange tried to fire, but he couldn't pull the trigger. Falling forward, he crashed into the mud, facedown.

Elizabeth cried out and ran from the boardwalk, her skirts dragging through the mud. She kneeled and tried frantically to turn him. The crusty old stage driver, spitting tobacco, came to roll Grange over.

"Did you see that fast draw?" a man asked from the gathering crowd.

"Sure, he's a Darringer," another man responded.

Kneeling in the mud, Elizabeth removed a glove to brush the dirt and wet from Grange's face. She was crying.

Then, realizing there was nothing she could do, she slowly stood up and looked at Jess through angry tears.

"*You* killed him. *You* bury him."

Slowly, Jess holstered his gun, a silent prayer on his lips. Nothing hurt more than a moment like this.

Clinton moved forward. After checking the body, he said to Elizabeth, "I'm afraid we'll have to search his luggage."

"Don't bother," she said, wiping away her tears. "It's in his money belt."

Clinton removed the fat belt and checked it.

Inside were several thick wads of greenbacks and some heavy gold coins.

"You stayin' for the funeral?" Clinton asked her.

"No," she said firmly.

"But he was your brother."

"He was my husband, Marshal. Oh, yes, I know," she said, turning to look up at Lorena. "He asked you to marry him. Well, all he wanted was your money. Don't you see? It was me he loved. Just me."

There was a long, awkward silence. Then she turned to look at Jess. Softening, she moved toward him and placed her hand on his arm.

"I liked you, Jess," she said.

Rising on her tiptoes, her hand on his neck, she pulled his face down to hers and kissed him on the lips. Her sweetness had returned, but for just a moment. When she turned to look down at her dead husband, she was a cold stranger again. She brushed the mud from her skirts and walked with dignity toward the stage.

Coming up the street, the judge was shaking his head.

"Darringer, I had better leave town before you get into any more trouble."

"He was acting as my deputy," Clinton assured him.

"Put it in writing," the judge said, shaking their hands.

The judge then joined Elizabeth alongside the stage. Smiling, and with her dark eyes flashing, she turned to him. Obliging, he helped her climb the small metal steps. He paused to drink in her loveliness before boarding. The nervous couple reappeared, boarded, and closed the door behind them.

Jess and Clinton watched the coach move away. Elizabeth was at the window, gazing back at them, lifting her hand in a slight farewell to Jess.

"You figure you have all Grange's ill-gotten fortune?" Jess asked.

"No, I don't."

"You goin' after her?"

"No, I'm not."

"You figure the judge will help her out?"

"It's a long way to Denver," Clinton said.

Jess grinned at the lawman, who refused to grin back.

The barber arrived to collect Grange's body. Lance Colby came over to Jess. "Now that this is all over," the rancher said, "I'd like you and your brother to stay on."

"No, thanks," Jess said. "I came for only one reason. But I appreciate the offer."

He shook Colby's hand, but refused to look up the steps at Lorena. Instead, he walked away, toward the jail. It seemed to take forever to get there. Inside, he closed the door in relief. The Hatcher brothers were sulking in their cells. Sam was sitting at the desk, his feet up.

"I saw you get Grange," Sam said. "Reckon you were right about him."

"He was taking the money, all right. But it seems that Elizabeth was his wife."

"Nice fellow. Now what?"

"You go to Hack and Harley's funeral for me," Jess said. "I'll watch the jail."

"Hey, that young lady must really have you on the run."

"We're gettin' out of here first thing in the morning. You can't trust any woman, Sam. One minute they're sweet and all kisses. The next, well, you saw Elizabeth."

"You got to admit they ain't boring," Sam said.

And so it was that Jess and Sam spent the night in the jail with Clinton, not wanting to be near the hotel. Jess sang and played trail songs, trying to remind himself that he wanted to be back on the cattle trail in the spring.

An hour before dawn, they made up their bedrolls and then Jess picked up his squeeze-box. Clinton walked out into the dark with them. It was cold.

"So where do you go from here?" Clinton asked.

"Sam's goin' back to Texas," Jess said.

Sam was disappointed, but he nodded agreement. "Right after I take a ride up into them mountains. But where are you going, Jess?"

"There's a lot of prairie out there," Jess said. "I got a lot of thinkin' to do. But I'll pick you up in Texas, around March. I'd be mighty proud to hit the cattle trail with you."

Sam grinned, pleased, as Jess turned to shake Clinton's hand.

The brothers said good-bye to the lawman and headed down the street to the livery. Inside, the lanterns were turned low. They heard the snoring of some men in the loft. Walking to the back entrance, they saddled up Comanche and Sam's sorrel. The stallion was prancing, ready to stretch its legs.

"You might be sorry you're not stickin' around to be with Lorena," Sam told him, without mentioning how Jess had once ridden away from Sue Ellen.

"Wouldn't do me any good," Jess told him. "Her pa figures I'm not good enough for her."

"Then you were considerin'—"

"I was doing no such thing," Jess growled.

"Then why don't you have the guts to say good-bye?"

Jess ignored him as they mounted and rode out the back toward a side gate. Dawn was fast approaching.

As Jess leaned down to open the gate, he nearly fell off the stallion. Lorena was standing there with a Winchester aimed right at his head. She was in her riding clothes and a heavy coat. Her golden hair glistened as if the dew had caressed it.

"Don't move," she said.

"What are you doing here?" he asked.

"I came to stop you. Get off that horse."

"What for?"

"You stole from my father. Now get off."

Dismayed, Jess slowly dismounted, as did Sam. They left the horses inside the corral and closed the gate. Lorena backed off, still aiming at Jess.

"Now march," she said. "Back to the jail."

"What did we steal?" Jess asked.

"You'll find out."

Jess wondered why he was letting this slip of a girl herd him back with a rifle. He could easily take it away from her. Or could he? He suddenly remembered that she was a dead shot.

The brothers walked around the livery, Lorena following. Lance Colby met them in front of the building. He also had a rifle. It was nearly daylight, the sky red in the east. It was cold, but Jess's face was hot.

"What's this all about?" he asked.

"Seems like you robbed me of somethin' I can't do without," Colby said.

"What's that?" Jess asked.

"Seems like my daughter wanted to run off

with you, but I told her it'd be much better if you just stayed. We can have the wedding as soon as she makes this dress she's got in mind."

"Wedding?" Jess echoed.

Slowly, he turned to look at Lorena. She was still holding the rifle, the butt pressed to her cheek, aiming at Jess.

"That thing loaded?" he asked.

Lowering it, she shook her head. She wasn't smiling. She was just standing there, beautiful, her golden hair glistening in the first light of the sun.

"I'm sorry," she said. "It was a foolish thing to do, but you're so hard-headed, Jess Darringer. I had to shock you into realizing you want to marry me."

"No such thing," Jess said.

"But you dived into the creek to save my life," she reminded him.

Sam and Colby were grinning. Jess was shaking.

"Look," Jess said, fighting for breath. "I can't marry any woman. I have a lot of wandering to do."

"Then I'll go with you," she said.

"No, you can't. Your father's already lost two sons."

"Then we'll both stay."

"Your mother won't approve of me," he said.

"She'll love you," Colby promised. "She likes folks what need improvement."

"You said I was just a gunfighter," Jess argued.

"You've proved to be a lot more'n that."

"What about Neal?" Jess asked Lorena. "He loves you."

"He's going to be all right. He's already talking about marrying Auralie Hatcher."

"I got nothin' to offer," Jess pointed out. "Just a few hundred dollars saved up. Not even enough to get a spread."

"You'll have a section of our place," Colby told him. "Along with Lorena's mine."

Cornered, Jess fumbled for a defense. "I'm a restless man," he said.

He turned and walked away, trying to breathe. He reached the boardwalk and stopped. He was torn in half, wanting to run and wanting to stay. Freedom and the lure of the distant, lone prairies were pulling at him.

The scent of lilac told him that Lorena was at his side. Shivers ran up his back.

Slowly, he turned and looked down at her. The early sunlight was turning her hair into shimmering, spun gold. Her eyes were the dark blue of a mountain lake. She was soft, vulnerable, brave. He thought of how she had dived into the creek, nearly drowning, preventing the outlaws' escape. He remembered her fight to stay alive in the canyon when they had first met. Just being near her was shattering. There was no other woman like her. No one before her had ever had him this close to disaster. He swallowed hard, his throat as dry as sand. His feet said to run. His heart, bursting with need for her, was fighting his good sense.

"What if I stay," he said, "and then get restless?"

"You won't," she assured him. "Because we're going to have a lot of children. You'll be very busy, Jess Darringer. But if you need to go sit under the stars some night, you'll have a big share of more than a few thousand acres to do it in. You might even take your sons along."

Jess knew he was lost. His knees were jelly. The only thing he could do was watch her move toward him. He suddenly reached for her, drew her into his arms, and crushed her against him, his lips finding hers in a kiss that made them both shiver with delight.

Leaning back in his arms, she smiled, breathless.

"But I'll be the boss," he said.

"Of course," she whispered, with a giggle that left him wondering.